THE EXPLOITS
OF CAPTAIN O'HAGAN

THE EXPLOITS OF CAPTAIN O'HAGAN

BY
SAX ROHMER
Author of "The Yellow Claw,"
"Dr. Fu Manchu," etc.

Bookfinger
New York City
1968

Portions of this book appeared serially in McClure's
Magazine during 1913-14

First Printed, Jarrolds, London,
December, 1916

First American Edition

A NECESSARY FOREWORD.

In presenting for perusal a selection of private notes dealing with the sometimes eccentric doings of my gallant friend and compatriot, Captain the Hon. Bernard O'Hagan, V.C., D.S.O., I desire in the first place to assure my reader that O'Hagan is in no degree related to anyone else of the name.

Recent circumstances have led him to resume military duties; but the splendid response of Democracy to the trumpet-call " Pro Patriâ " has in no way unsettled his singular opinions. In the face of evidence to the contrary which many regard as conclusive, he maintains that the ideal form of government is government by an absolute monarchy.

It forms no part of my plan either to

support or to seek to disprove the theories of Captain O'Hagan. In justice to my distinguished friend, I must add that support and opposition alike are matters of indifference to him. He stands alone—aloof—aloft. Neither as apologist nor as eulogist do I pen these lines, but merely as the chronicler of remarkable events in the career of a remarkable man.

EXPLOIT THE FIRST.
HE PATRONISES PAMELA

EXPLOIT THE FIRST.

HE PATRONISES PAMELA.

I.

THE HAT OF MR. PARKINS.

A VERY wilderness is Bernard O'Hagan, which no man could hope thoroughly to explore; a most picturesque figure in the satin-lined cloak which he loves to wear in defiance of fashion and indeed of civilised custom, singularly resembling the Merry Monarch whom a lady of his race once entertained right regally at the ancestral home of the O'Hagans. The unexpectedness of the man is one of the most marked features of his character—the one that makes his society at once delightful and alarming.

"My boy," he will burst out, as we sit in a crowded café, "that gentleman yonder is unduly interested in my appearance." And, stepping over to the offensive one: "Sir, you are staring at me. I suspect you of being a bum-bailiff!"

"What!" says the other, in all probability —whilst, my friend and I the observed of many observers, I tremble for the outcome of the affair—" how dare you! Damn it! how dare you!"

"Because," replies O'Hagan, with a sort of calm ferocity, "I desire to pull your nose, and only await a fitting opportunity! You are a puppy, sir! There is my card!"

The man leaps in anger to his feet. Others arise, too, and waiters approach.

"You will regret this outrage!" says the man, pale or inflamed. "You will hear from my solicitor!"

Then O'Hagan throws back his picturesque head and laughs.

"The solicitor again!" he cries, snapping his fingers. "Always the solicitor—or the police! Is there no man alive to-day who can fight his own battles?"

He quietly returns to his table. The

HE PATRONISES PAMELA 13

other speaks to the manager, and, if he be a good customer, the manager comes across to O'Hagan. O'Hagan rises slowly, fixing his eyes upon him. And, somehow, O'Hagan is never ejected. A devil of a fellow.

To the charge that he is a polished kind of bully he will reply calmly, arguing that he is merely of a sensitive and aristocratic temperament and suffers affront where one more callous would be conscious of none. He will submit to rudeness from no man, be he premier or potman; yet he is never vulgarly embroiled.

O'Hagan rarely wears a hat during the day. There is a simple explanation. At one time in his chequered career, the only presentable hat he possessed was a crush-hat. It was then that he cultivated the hatless fashion. This habit of going hatless directly led to his meeting with Pamela.

Captain O'Hagan was walking along a crowded, shop-lined thoroughfare, with that swinging stride which he will tell you runs in the family, and which enabled his ancestor Patrick to secure enrolment in the ranks of the Musketeers of Louis XIII. Before the door of a newsagent's establishment—quite an unpretentious little shop—two men stood. One of them, elderly, waved a tweed cap to a girl more than ordinarily pretty who was making her way up the steps to the roof of a moving motor bus. The girl carried a neat brown leather case, and, having gained a seat, turned and waved her handkerchief. The younger man smiled sourly, but did not join the elder in his waving.

O'Hagan, delighted with the girl's animation and beauty, halted by the two, smiling at the retreating figure. Quite mechanically he raised the hard felt hat from the head of the younger and less enthusiastic man, and waved it with a vigour even more marked than that of the elder waver.

He was recalled to the scene from which the girl now had disappeared amid the motley traffic, by a violent punch in the ribs.

"Blighter!" said a coarse voice. "My 'at!"

Another than Captain O'Hagan had turned quickly, with arm raised to ward off another

HE PATRONISES PAMELA

possible blow. But with O'Hagan the cult of the unusual is a creed to which he sacrifices daily. Some difficulty he experienced in suppressing a gasp, but he turned unhastily, calmly, and looked into the bright little eyes of the hat's owner. These were set upon him wickedly, and a truculent, blue-shaded jaw was thrust forward in menace.

"You've properly asked for it," continued the man, tensely, "and you're goin' to get it!"

"Jem!" protested the older man, fearfully. "Not here——"

Straight from the shoulder a piston stroke was launched at O'Hagan. It was a blow with brawn to drive it, with science to direct it. It was aimed—and well—in accordance with ring traditions of the "knock-out." But one who takes unwarrantable liberties with unknowns' hats must be prepared for reprisals.

O'Hagan is fond of showing his friends the tricks learned of Shashu Myuku of Nagasaki; he is equally prompt to demonstrate them to others. Without employing his right hand, which was engaged in holding the felt hat, he struck down the impending blow (any but a pupil of Myuku must have endeavoured to strike it *up*), thrust his left foot rapidly against his opponent's advanced right shin, and, by a simple process of natural law the pugilist pitched forward on to the pavement, propelled by all the force of his own attacking impetus.

Much shaken, and with a rivulet of blood trickling down his nose from a damaged forehead, he got upon his feet again. Captain O'Hagan deliberately hurled the bowler far out into the stream of traffic, and fixed his large eyes upon its white-faced owner.

"One word," he said, in that tone of suppressed ferocity wholly inimitable, "and I will throw you after it! You ape!"

The dazed and much-insulted man glanced from a shapeless dark mass which, prior to the passage of a brewer's traction-engine, had been a felt hat, to the face of O'Hagan; and began with his handkerchief to wipe blood from his wounds. O'Hagan cast his eyes upward to the legend: "J. Crichton,

HE PATRONISES PAMELA

Newsagent," and took the elder man by the arm.

"A word with you, Mr. Crichton!" he said, sweeping that astonished old tradesman into the shop, and ignoring the knot of interested spectators gathered at the door.

II.

"THE ART OF GENTLE THOUGHT."

A CHAIR stood by the journal-strewn counter.

"Sit down," said O'Hagan kindly, "and answer a few questions! Who is that person whose hat I honoured?"

The newsagent, who momentarily was expecting to awaken from this bad dream, shook his head ominously.

"It's Jem Parkins, sir," he replied, with that respect bordering upon awe which O'Hagan inspires in the plebeian soul. "He's got the *Blue Dragon* now, but he's ex-middleweight champion. There'll be the devil to pay when he's pulled hisself together, sir!"

"Reserve your speculations, Mr. Crichton," said O'Hagan, "and confine yourself to facts. The young lady on the bus—your daughter?"

"Yes, sir."

"She takes after her mother."

Mr. Crichton stared.

"Did you know Polly—Mrs. Crichton, sir?"

"No. I was referring to your daughter's good looks. She dresses neatly."

Mr. Crichton had something of the British tradesman's independent spirit, and even the awe inspired by O'Hagan's tremendous presence could not wholly smother his paternal resentment.

"I'd have you know that Pamela's a lady, sir! And I'd have——"

"Pamela is quite an unusual name for a girl of the lower classes. In what way is Parkins interested?"

The mild eye of Mr. J. Crichton smouldered into faint flame.

"The lower classes! The——"

"I asked you a question."

Mr. Crichton hesitated, glanced around

HE PATRONISES PAMELA

his shop—his *own* shop—noted that his pugilistic friend was entering the door with an air of business-like truculence, and took his elusive courage in both hands.

"I decline to be cross-examined—by you—or—by——"

Mr. Parkins closed the shop-door, bolted it, and pulled down the blue blind. He began deliberately to remove his coat.

"Half a mo, Mr. C.," he interrupted in a quivering voice. "Sorry to put you out, but it's got to be done. I'll smash 'im; then you can call for the police and give 'im in charge!"

O'Hagan raised the monocle swung upon the broad black ribbon, and holding it at some distance from his right eye, surveyed the speaker.

"I thought I forbade you to address me?" he remarked icily.

Parkins, removing a collar and shirt-front combined, began to whistle.

"I'll show you—comin' buttin' in and runnin' after respectable girls!" he announced hoarsely. "*Blighter!*"

O'Hagan dropped the monocle and laid his cane upon the counter At the moment that Parkins stood upright and squared his chest, the Captain snatched up Mr. Crichton', day-book—a heavy, leather-bound volume—and hurled it full at the pugilist's head. One of the precepts of the Higher Jiu-Jitsu, or " Art of Gentle Thought," he will tell you, is to avail yourself of any missile within reach. His aim, then, is deadly. The day-book struck Parkins edgewise across the face, felling him like a stricken bullock—felling him utterly, brutally.

He crashed into the corner by the door—and lay still. (" A dreadful blow was struck at every gentleman when the sword was taken from him," O'Hagan will say. " One cannot soil one's gloves with the blood of churls.")

" If you compel me to deal with you" said the Captain, as Parkins returned to groaning consciousness of his injuries, " I shall cut your ears off! "

Do not judge my friend harshly. He was born three centuries too late, that is all.

HE PATRONISES PAMELA

The claim of Democracy to an equality with Aristocracy is as unintelligible to him as it must have been to Denis O'Hagan, who upheld the Stuart cause whilst he had breath, and died at last like a gentleman at Worcester, having demonstrated his distaste for plebeian company by personally dispatching seven Roundheads. Or perhaps the autocratic soul of Patrick O'Hagan lives again within Bernard. This member of the family, sometime of the *Mousquetaires du roi*, narrowly escaped the Bastille for decapitating a Paris grocer who insulted a lady and attaching the erring tradesman's head to his own shop-sign.

Parkins dizzily strove to get upon his feet. Mr. Crichton, trembling, was seeking to reach the telephone.

"Sit down, Mr. Crichton," directed O'Hagan, turning the monocle upon him.

"This is my shop—and that's one o' my friends——"

"Sit down, Mr. Crichton."

Mr. Crichton sat down.

"You"—to the tottering pugilist—"put on your filthy rags, and get out."

Parkins steadied himself against the door.

"What d'you mean, get out? I've got more right 'ere than you! Just wait, you cowardly skunk! I'll 'ave you yet! I'll quod you for this!"

"You have one minute to get out. If I hear from you again, I shall give you in charge for assault and battery!"

O'Hagan, lolling against the counter, swung the monocle carelessly. The amplitude of his nonchalance prevailed. Parkins, recalling that he had struck the first blow, stuffed his "dicky" into his coat, resumed that garment, and began to unbolt the door.

With never a backward glance, the discredited Mr. Parkins made his exit. One of a curious group, without, entered on the pretence of buying a halfpenny paper. He was served by the trembling newsagent, but save for the presence of a hatless, distinguished gentleman, saw nothing to satisfy his curiosity in Mr. Crichton's shop.

"Now, Mr. Crichton," said O'Hagan, the customer departed, "in reference to Pamela: has the fellow, Parkins, pretensions?"

HE PATRONISES PAMELA

Mr. Crichton, *pro tempore*, was past protest.

"He's an old pal o' mine," he explained, unsteadily, "and well off—and——"

"Pamela does not approve him?"

"Well, she's got such superior ideas. But Parkins——"

"It is out of the question, Crichton. Dismiss the idea. Mrs. Crichton was a woman of higher social standing than yourself?"

The newsagent felt suffocation to be an imminent danger.

"She was the daughter of a lit'r'y gentleman——"

"Singular that she should have married you! Her father was badly in debt, possibly?"

"Look here ——!"

"I say, possibly the late Mrs. Crichton's father was financially indebted to you?"

Crichton, cowed:

"I pretty well kept him, for years!"

"Ah! poor girl! A tragedy of poverty! But you have not neglected Pamela's education?"

"She's had the best that money could give her!"

O'Hagan seized the hand of the bewildered Mr. Crichton and wrung it warmly.

"There are redeeming features in your character, Crichton!" he said. "For your endeavours on the girl's behalf I can forgive you much. Rely upon my friendship! And Pamela has literary inclinations?"

"No, sir," answered the newsagent, whose world was being turned topsy-turvy, who alternately believed that he was in the company of a madman or that he himself was mad. "She's a musician; I've had her properly taught; she composes!"

Above all the chaos reigning in his mind, paternal pride asserted its sovereignty and his voice proclaimed it.

"Ah! composes? She has just gone to see a publisher? She had music in the leather case?"

"Her new piece, sir. She reckons it's goin' to make her!"

"What has she published?"

Mr. Crichton, crestfallen:

HE PATRONISES PAMELA

"Nothing, sir! You see, she's unknown. They won't give her a chance."

"She will return to lunch?"

The newsagent stared.

"Pamela 'll be home to dinner!" he said.

"The midday meal? Exactly. I will lunch with you, Crichton. My name is Captain O'Hagan."

His mode of patronage was superb, incomparable.

III.

PAMELA RETURNS.

PAMELA arrived late, a dainty figure in her neat serge costume; but the very curl that floated across her brow, the limp little hand that held the music-case, spoke of dejection. Her charming face was not habitually pale, O'Hagan felt assured, nor were such glorious eyes meant to be dimmed with threatening tears.

"Hullo, Pam!" began her father heartily—and hesitated. "Why—won't they take it?"

A forlorn little shake of the head.

"That horrible Ritzmann offered to publish it—if I would let him have it for nothing!"

"For nothing! Didn't he offer to pay anything?"

"Not after I had declined to go to lunch with him!"

Pamela laughed; not mirthfully.

"Cheer up, Pam," said Mr. Crichton, in a voice of abysmal gloom. "A—er—a friend——"

"A friend, yes, Crichton," interrupted O'Hagan. "Don't be nervous."

"A friend of mine—*Captain* O'Hagan—has called to see us!"

Pamela blushed delightfully; O'Hagan bowed inimitably.

"Didn't Mr.—Parkins—stay?"

Crichton coughed.

"He couldn't stop, after all!" he replied.

HE PATRONISES PAMELA

Pamela removed her hat. "Good job, too," she muttered under her breath.

And then began that singular repast, throughout which O'Hagan talked as only O'Hagan can talk; talked himself into the hearts of the Crichtons. The old man's natural resentment—which hitherto had not become wholly dispersed—melted before the geniality of his distinguished guest; Mr. Parkins was forgotten. Pamela forgot her troubles and became all smiles. Crichton burned with pride to note that Captain O'Hagan treated her as an intellectual equal. Of the Captain's honourable and friendly intentions no man could doubt after thirty minutes in his company; and so that was a happy hour spent at the newsagent's humble table.

The meal despatched:

"Now for the music!" said O'Hagan, and crossing the little room, he opened the piano.

Pamela stared.

"May I try over your new piece, Miss Crichton?"

"Oh!" cried the girl. "You play?"

"A little. I should like, as a pleasure, to hear your own rendering; as a matter of business I should prefer to play the piece myself."

"A matter of business――"

"You hope to place these compositions?"

"Oh!" said Pamela blankly; "yes," and took the MS. from her music-case, adjusting it upon the piano-rack.

Few people have heard O'Hagan play the piano. He never plays unless requested and the many being ignorant of his accomplishment, he rarely is requested. But from the moment that his long, white fingers caressed the keys in the opening bar until that when they leapt back from the final chord, his audience of two listened spellbound. The piece was a delicate, feminine morsel; individual, charming; upon an elusive melody, which haunted the ear, which spelt Popularity. For a moment there was silence. O'Hagan swung around and faced Pamela.

"Miss Crichton," he said, "you will make

HE PATRONISES PAMELA

a large sum of money with your music. One day you will be famous."

Pamela blushed; her lips trembled. She had never heard her dainty composition played before by hands other than her own. It was something of a revelation to its composer—this rippling, fascinating cascade of harmony which had flown out under the subtle touch of the visitor. Tears were not far from her eyes again.

"Give me more of your pieces—all you can find," directed O'Hagan.

Glad enough of an excuse to hide her emotion, the girl ran to a little escretoire and took out six or seven neatly-written compositions. O'Hagan placed them before him, and played through them all, without hesitation, without error; with intense sympathy and understanding. Soon she was beside him, turning over the familiar pages; her wayward curls brushed his cheek. When the master-touch had sounded the finale of the last piece, old Crichton pulled out a handkerchief and blew his nose in clarion fashion.

"What terms were you asking of—er—Ritzmann?" said the Captain abruptly.

"The usual ten per cent.," replied Pamela, "with—something on account."

"How much on account?"

"Ritzmann, I have heard—I know—usually gives ten guineas."

She spoke the words with awe. Ten guineas on account of a composition of *hers*—of her very own! It was a dream!

"Ah! Ten guineas on account of a ten per cent. royalty? Let me see: we have eight pieces here. Can you find two more?"

"There is a suite of three short numbers."

"Bring that."

Pamela found it, and brought it. O'Hagan played it, and was delighted.

"Four sharps," he criticised, "are bad in a composition designed for general popularity. Would it lose by transposition into a more simple key?"

"I think not," said Pamela.

"Well," continued O'Hagan, "it is a matter for discussion later. May I take these with me?"

HE PATRONISES PAMELA

" Of course ! " said Pamela.   " But——"

" Can you give me until Thursday to place them for you ? "

" To place them ! To place *all* of them ? "

" All of them ! Can you give me until Thursday ? "

Pamela's pretty eyes were widely staring.

" You overwhelm me ! Do you really mean it ? "

" Will you wait until Thursday and see ? "

" Of course ! " said Pamela.

IV.

A MUSICAL INTERLUDE.

O'HAGAN entered my rooms with the impressive dignity of a Richelieu ; in the very distinction of the man there is something opulent. His refined *insouciance* surpasses anything of the kind one could imagine.

" Will you do me a trifling service, Raymond ? "

"Consider it as done."

He threw himself into the blue Chesterfield lounge with the native grace no lesser man could hope to imitate. His pose suggested that a rapier hung at his hip and must be taken into consideration. A plumed hat would have struck no discordant note but merely have harmonised with the purple-lined cloak. O'Hagan's head one might surmise to be from a study by Van Dyck.

"I am running around to Ritzmann's, the music-publishers, in Berners Street."

Now, I noted that he carried a full portfolio.

"At last you have decided to enter the field? You do wisely."

"I am acting on behalf of a friend—a lady."

"Indeed. What part do I play?"

"Come along. I will explain."

We walked up Oxford Street to the corner of Berners Street. O'Hagan creates a sensation wherever he appears: I am hardened to this.

"You will reconnoitre, Raymond. You

HE PATRONISES PAMELA 33

will send in a card—anybody's card but your own—to Mr. Paul Ritzmann."

" What ! "

" You are representing Messrs. Angelo Morris, of Monte Video ! Probably there is no such firm ; I invented the name. You are prepared to handle Ritzmann's dance-catalogue throughout the southern continent. If he declines to do business, no matter ; if he is interested, make an appointment at your hotel—the Savoy sounds substantial without being gaudy."

" What is the object of this mendacity ? "

" To learn if there is a second door to Ritzmann's office ; another than that opening on the shop. If there is, come out by it at all costs, and note where it leads you to. I think, and hope, it will open on a corridor communicating with the street. From what I know of Ritzmann I feel confident that there will be such a private entrance. You will note, also, where the *other* end of this hypothetical passage leads to. Probably it will be to a stair. Finally, you will report respecting the occupant of the suite of offices above—the suite to which this stair should conduct you."

"I am not confident," I said; "but I will do my best."

Three minutes later I was ushered into the Semitic presence of Mr. Paul Ritzmann. Mr. Ritzmann had a corpulent person, a bald head, and an oily smile. He wore diamond rings on his left hand as well as on his right, by which token I knew that he was really rich. A Hebrew of the Ritzmann type buys a diamond ring as soon as he can afford it, and displays it upon his right hand. That is an advertising investment; it signifies that he is ambitious. But when his right hand is full and he begins to adorn his left it implies that his ambition is realised.

He made no plunge at my South American offer. He was very cautious.

"I will give you a ring at the hotel, Mr. Eddington." (I had sent in the card of Harry Eddington, who at the time was with an expedition looking for the South Pole.) "I dare say we may be able to fix something up."

HE PATRONISES PAMELA 35

" Good morning."

I made a plunge for a door on the left of his desk.

" This way out, Mr. Eddington," came after me ; but I was in the corridor, and closed the door behind me.

A white hand with extended fingers was painted on the further wall, and, beneath it, the words :

> HARRIS & HARRIS,
> *Domestic Employment Agency.*

Turning to the right, I passed out into Berners Street.

" It is well," said O'Hagan, musingly, when I had made my report. " You will now get back to the said corridor, without permitting yourself to be seen from Ritzmann's shop ; you will wait by Ritzmann's private door, but on the stair side, so that when I come out he won't notice you. I shall hand you something ; you will go up Harris and Harris's stair like a rocket, concealing, of course, the object referred to, and see about a cook. Then go home."

One pays for the privilege of O'Hagan's friendship.

I had not been at my post more than half a minute, when I saw O'Hagan pass in the street and enter the Ritzmann shop. I began to make notes in a note-book to excuse my loitering. Leaving me so engaged, you will please follow the Captain.

To a counter-clerk:

"Kindly inform Mr. Ritzmann," he said, "that the gentleman he is expecting will see him."

"Yes, sir. Certainly, sir. Will you take a seat!"

This, the shop staff were decided, was either a distinguished Russian composer or a gentleman of title interested in a new musical comedy for the "Gaiety."

A moment later:

"Mr. Ritzmann will see you at once, sir. This way, if you please."

O'Hagan swung grandly office-ward, and entered to find Ritzmann standing to greet him.

The clerk was about to retire.

HE PATRONISES PAMELA 37

"My good fellow," called O'Hagan, "Mr. Ritzmann and I are not to be interrupted upon any account."

The clerk bowed and retired. Ritzmann stared.

"You say I was expecting you, Mr.——?"

O'Hagan smiled, waving his hand reassuringly.

"Pray be seated, Mr. Ritzmann."

Mr. Ritzmann accepted the invitation, and O'Hagan sat upon the edge of the desk facing him. O'Hagan was between Mr. Ritzmann and the bell.

"I have decided to place with you for immediate publication a parcel of charming compositions—nine in all."

Ritzmann's eyes began to protrude.

"They are these."

O'Hagan opened the portfolio and set the heap of MSS. on the desk.

With frequent sideway glances at his extraordinary visitor, Mr. Ritzmann began to look at the music.

"Why," he burst out, suddenly, pushing the whole of it towards the Captain, "all this stuff has been submitted by post, and declined! All but this thing; and Miss Crichton was here only the other day with it. I don't want the junk, my dear sir! If I'd known that's what you——"

O'Hagan waved him to silence.

"Of all these things I am fully aware, Mr. Ritzmann; but I thought I had explained that I had selected you to publish these compositions?"

The other clutched the arms of his chair.

"*Selected* me?"

"That was my expression. Had the music been worthless——"

"It *is* worthless! Piffle!"

"Had the music been worthless I should not have offered it to you. But each of these nine items is a sound speculation. We shall require nine agreement-forms."

Ritzmann, staring, rose slowly to his feet.

"Sit down, Mr. Ritzmann."

Ritzmann moistened his thick lips preparatory to comment.

"Sit down, Mr. Ritzmann."

He sat down; and his fleshy hands were

HE PATRONISES PAMELA

not quite steady; the diamonds danced and sparkled. He managed to achieve coherent speech:

"This is a damn big bluff! But if you bluff from now——"

"You have royalty-forms in your desk; we shall require nine."

Ritzmann got on his feet and plunged for the bell. He was hurled back with violence; and his eyes protruded unnaturally at sight of the pistol which pointed at his bald skull.

"Nine forms, Mr. Ritzmann."

"You must—be mad. You—dare not——"

"There you are in error. I would shoot you without compunction. If I failed to escape I should shoot myself. I have nothing to live for, and I should go to eternity with that one good deed to my credit. I will dictate the titles of the nine pieces and you will fill in the forms."

Ritzmann's face grew ashy. He looked a stricken man. The bundle of forms shook and rustled like autumn leaves in a breeze. Unemotionally, O'Hagan read out the titles;

shakily, all but illegibly, the publisher wrote them in. Form after form was filled up, dated and signed. Two, O'Hagan rejected as quite illegible. But at last he was satisfied, and pocketed the nine.

"Ten guineas on account of each," he said; "that will be a cheque for ninety-four pounds, ten shillings, payable to Miss Pamela Crichton."

Ritzmann's face showed that he was contemplating rebellion.

"I shall count ten, Mr. Ritzmann!"

The cheque was drawn up and signed. O'Hagan carefully folded and placed it in his pocket-book.

"Good day," he said, and backed towards the door.

He opened it and stepped out into the passage. He had not closed it ere with bell and husky voice Ritzmann was summoning assistance.

O'Hagan handed me the pistol. He took out his cigarette-case and selected a cigarette. Before he had found his matchbox I was upstairs and inside Messrs. Harris and Harris's

HE PATRONISES PAMELA 41

office. It must have been at about the moment when I was stating my lack of a suitable parlourmaid, that three clerks, rushing out of the shop, intercepted the Captain, as, match in hand, he stood at the street-end of the passage.

They would have seized him; but O'Hagan's eyes can quell.

"Your dirty hands off! The meaning of this outrage?"

Trembling, grey-faced, Mr. Ritzmann joined the three clerks. A fourth, who had been detailed to that duty, returned from an adjacent corner with a constable.

"Arrest that man! He has robbed me!"

O'Hagan closed his matchbox with a *click* and fixed his eyes upon the officer.

"Constable," he said, with dignity, "step into the shop. This is an outrage for which Mr. Ritzmann shall pay. Step inside if you please—all of you."

The wide-eyed clerks returned to the shop. Ritzmann, never taking his gaze from O'Hagan, but keeping at a safe distance, entered behind the Captain, clutching at

the perplexed policeman and whispering:
"He has robbed me! He's got my cheque
in his pocket!"

Having entered the shop,—to the excited
clerks:

"Return to your duties, good fellows!'
ordered O'Hagan. "I am not accustomed
to be made an object of vulgar curiosity!
Mr. Ritzmann, lead the way to your office.
Constable—follow."

The odd trio entered Ritzmann's sanctum.
O'Hagan closed the door.

"He's dangerous!" cried the publisher.
"He carries a pistol!"

O'Hagan raised his hand.

"The officer, Mr. Ritzmann," he said,
"is prepared to do his duty. But you
have not stated your case. Of what am I
accused?"

"Of extorting money from me, at the
point of a pistol!"

"Officer! You have my permission to
look for the weapon!"

The constable ran his hands over O'Hagan.

"Excuse me, sir," he reported to Mr.

HE PATRONISES PAMELA 43

Ritzmann, who was now regaining colour and perspiring freely, " but the gentleman hasn't got any pistol on him!"

" He's dropped it in the passage!" yelled Ritzmann. " He——"

Again O'Hagan raised the forceful hand.

" One of your clerks can go and look; and would you be good enough to request your manager to join us?"

The necessary instructions were given, and the manager appeared. O'Hagan threw down his bunch of agreements and displayed the cheque.

" Sir," he said to the manager, " are these in order?"

" He made me do it!" cried Ritzmann hoarsely, " at the point of a pistol!"

A shopman entered to report that there was no pistol in the passage. Ritzmann began to swear.

" Silence!" thundered O'Hagan. " Silence! you contemptible scoundrel!" To the manager: " Are those agreements and this cheque quite regular?"

" Well," said the manager, glancing deprecatingly at his employer—" I can see nothing irregular about them. They are in your writing, Mr. Ritzmann!"

"He held a pistol to my head!" cried the publisher. "You're a pack of fools! Fools! Officer! will you do your duty and arrest that thief!"

O'Hagan took a stride towards the speaker.

"Stop him!" quavered Ritzmann, paling. "He——"

"Mr. Ritzmann," said O'Hagan calmly, "you are a low blackguard! Repenting of your bargain, you invented this cock-and-bull story as a means of evading it! Knowing me to be a man who has led an adventurous life, you thought yourself safe in charging me with carrying arms! I have several witnesses to the fact that you have grossly slandered me. That your charge is absurd—insane—worthy of a 'penny-dreadful'—renders it none the less slanderous. You will either apologise, here and now, or—there is my card. My solicitor will take charge of the matter in the morning!"

Down on to the desk before the bewildered

HE PATRONISES PAMELA

Ritzmann, O'Hagan cast his card. Like everything appertaining to that remarkable man, his card is impressive, unusual, striking; a battery. Mr. Ritzmann, his manager and the constable, read the following:

Capt. the Hon Bernard O'Hagan,
V.C., D.S.O.

Junior Guards' Club.

The constable stood stiffly to attention, and saluted.

"What am I to do, sir?" he asked—of O'Hagan.

"Ring up Gerrard 04385!"

Ritzmann dropped into his chair and sat there with bulging eyes. The constable, amid a surprising silence, took up the telephone and got the desired number.

"Ask if that is the Junior Guards," directed O'Hagan.

Yes, it was the Junior Guards.

"See if Colonel Sir Gerald Fitz Ayre is in the house."

The name of that celebrated soldier electrified the Captain's audience. Fitz Ayre was found and came to the telephone. O'Hagan took the receiver from the now extremely respectful officer.

"That you, Fitz Ayre? Yes; O'Hagan speaking. My confounded eccentricities of costume have got me into hot water again! Will you please *describe me* to the person who is now coming to the 'phone! Yes. Thank you."

Ritzmann, summoned imperiously, took the receiver in his trembling hands. But he did not listen to the Colonel's florid description of O'Hagan's person; for his mind was otherwise engaged. He knew himself the victim of a tremendous bluff, but, now, he knew the bluffer for one above his reach; he knew, moreover, that he lacked evidence, and that he had been guilty of a slander which might cost him thousands. Pamela Crichton's music was quite saleable. He would lose nothing by the deal;

HE PATRONISES PAMELA 47

he would see to that. His course was clear.

"Thanks. Good-bye."

Ritzmann turned to O'Hagan.

"I apologise, Captain O'Hagan!" he said. "I was mad! Officer—a sovereign for you!"

* * * * *

"May I present my friend, Mr. Lawrence Raymond?" said O'Hagan. "This is Miss Pamela Crichton, the clever composer I spoke about! Isn't she a picture?"

She was. But she blushed furiously. O'Hagan handed her a bundle of agreements. As she looked through them, her flushed cheeks grew quite pale. When a cheque for ninety guineas was placed in her hands, frankly, I thought she would have swooned.

Old Crichton, hovering about in the dingy background, showed as a man who is dazed beyond comprehension.

"Oh, Captain O'Hagan," began Pamela, and her pretty eyes were troubled, "how can I thank you! Why have you done this—for *me*?"

"Because you are *you*, Pamela!" said O'Hagan. "Because you are so very charming, and because one day you will be so very famous!"

Pamela met his eyes frankly—and was content.

Throughout our brief stay, O'Hagan's treatment of the girl was worthy of the days of chivalry. Never, for a moment, did he presume upon that superiority of blood which is so real in his eyes, nor upon the service he had done this newsagent's daughter. When we took our leave he kissed her hand in his astonishing, cavalierly way, tactfully ignoring her sweet confusion, clapped her father patronisingly upon the back—and swung out of the shop, a gentleman full three hundred years behind his time—the only living being who has recovered the Grand Manner.

You would like to meet my friend O'Hagan.

EXPLOIT THE SECOND.

HE CLEARS THE COURSE FOR TRUE LOVE.

EXPLOIT THE SECOND.

HE CLEARS THE COURSE FOR TRUE LOVE.

I.

THE GLOOMY CAVALIER.

THAT class distinctions should be marked by insuperable barriers is a theory that amounts to a religion with O'Hagan. The *caste* system of India is delightful to his exclusiveness. I think, between patricians and plebeians, he would like to erect a series of stone hedges. To the voice of Democracy he is deaf, and would have a governing body selected from the oldest families in the kingdom.

"To-day," he will declare, "there are many gentlemen externally indistinguishable from grocers' assistants. I know dukes who look like head waiters, and head waiters who look like earls."

He throws back the folds of his astonishing satin-lined cloak, more fully to reveal its inner splendour.

"I, myself," he confides, "have been mistaken for an impresario, and once for a professional conjuror. I have repeatedly been compelled to thrash my man in order to check attempts at familiarity."

He sighs for the days when nobility unmistakably proclaimed itself; when an aristocrat was disgraced who dabbled in commerce and a tradesman castigated who raised his eyes above the level prescribed for him.

"A gentleman," says O'Hagan, "is never at a loss for the right word at the right time. He knows when to throw down the gauntlet, and when to apologise (to his equals). In this way, factitious gentility often is unmasked."

In support of this contention Captain O'Hagan will tell you a story.

One evening, at about seven o'clock, he chanced to be standing upon the corner of a prosperous suburban avenue in an exclusive, if slightly snob-ridden, district. An my memory serves me, he was waiting for a cab.

Merely to say that Captain O'Hagan stands upon a corner is to do poor justice to the verity. O'Hagan not only stands upon a corner; he occupies and ornaments it. With picturesque head, hatless, aloft—something of a rebuke to the Lady O'Hagan who was a contemporary of Charles II.—one gloved hand resting upon the heavy ebony cane, two fingers of the other dangling the large monocle, dependent on its black silk ribbon, his is a figure for long remembrance.

From the avenue came a lady escorted by a gentleman. The lady was young and pretty; her face peeped out from her wraps bewitchingly; and she carried one of those feminine sachet arrangements, in which, by the light of the street lamp, she anxiously searched. Her companion ransacked his overcoat pockets, his dress-coat pockets, his waistcoat and trousers pockets; and even looked in his crush-hat. When, following a hurried colloquy, he retraced his steps.

O'Hagan, his monocle held some three inches from his left eye, surveyed the charming figure, which now added a new beauty to the corner, with critical æsthetic appreciation. Do not suppose the attention a rude one. O'Hagan is incapable of rudeness to a woman. In another it had been rudeness— yes; but O'Hagan's frank interest, though embarrassing, is an exquisite flattery. His approval is a superb tribute.

He approved. The lady was not unaware of this, nor in the slightest degree displeased. Returning the forgetful cavalier, the pair moved away past the Captain. And two bright eyes acknowledged admiration with a discreet glance swift as a rapier thrust.

But Jealousy has as many heads and as many eyes as Siva; nor has it a lesser malignancy. The man turned; strode back to O'Hagan.

"What do you mean, sir, by staring at my friend in that way?"

His voice, his gaze, his attitude, were truculent. O'Hagan was delighted with such a display of spirit. He dropped the glass and bowed.

"If your friend has complained of me, sir, I shall never forgive myself."

"I await no complaint from her. *I* am complaining, confound your impudence!"

O'Hagan raised the glass again, measuring the depths of the speaker's resentment. He considered the words ill-chosen and ill-mannered; and instantly had revised his estimate of the speaker's character.

"An entirely different matter, sir," says he. "*You* can go to the devil."

The other flushed and thrust himself nearer to the suave Captain.

"You overdressed puppy!" he rapped furiously. "I have a mind to knock you down!"

Dropped the monocle; and a slip of pasteboard was thrust into the hand of the irate man.

"Your card, sir!" demanded O'Hagan. "At a more fitting time I will afford you every facility."

"I only exchange cards with gentlemen!' sneered the other, savagely; and tore into fragments the one he held.

"Your card, sir!" repeated O'Hagan sternly. "You have insulted me, and I demand an opportunity to reply to you. Your card, sir!"

"Be damned to you!" said the other—and walked off to rejoin the lady.

O'Hagan was but a pace later beside her. He bowed, as no man has bowed in England since the days of plumes and lace.

"Madam, permit me to offer you my most humble apologies for having annoyed you!"

Innocent eyes, with an imp of mischief dancing in their shadowed pools, met the Captain's.

"You are mistaken, sir. You have not annoyed me in the slightest!"

("She was a born coquette," O'Hagan has confided to me; "but devilish pretty and full of spirit. Too joyous a nature by far to dovetail with the sour-jowl who had insulted me.")

CLEARS COURSE FOR TRUE LOVE 57

"Then permit me to apologise for your friend," continued the amazing Captain, "who forces this necessity upon me by declining his card!"

"How dare you!" cried the friend, breathless. "Hang it all! I'll give you in charge if you continue to annoy me!"

"Your card, sir," persisted O'Hagan. "It is unavoidable that you afford me satisfaction for the insult placed upon me."

"Come along, Moira," breathed the enraged man, and offered his arm to the girl. "We shall be late for dinner. Never mind this lunatic!"

They proceeded. O'Hagan paced gloomily beside them. Some twenty yards thus; then:

"Clear out, confound you!" cried the man, turning upon O'Hagan with a leaping blaze of passion. "By heaven, you will make me forget myself!"

"You have done so already—for which reason I demand to know where I may find you."

Choking—wrought upon to the limit of

his endurance—the other stood, mouth a-twitch, hands clenched.

"Your card, sir," said O'Hagan icily.

The man addressed snatched again at the girl's arm and hurried her onward. Speech, now, was denied to him; his companion could feel how he quivered and shook in the gale of his emotions. Somewhat, she was frightened; but in part, too, the novelty of the situation pleased the romantic within her. She knew not what to say apposite to the strange impasse, so wisely said nothing.

Captain O'Hagan completed the silent trio.

Through a gate whose opening discovered a carriage-sweep they passed. Upon a neat lawn lights blazed out from every visible window of a substantial mansion. The obstinate and enraged stranger recovered command of his tongue.

"How dare you follow me into these premises!"

"I am not a spy, to follow any man," retorted O'Hagan. "I am *accompanying* you!"

CLEARS COURSE FOR TRUE LOVE 59

The bell's ring brought a trim maid. In the cosy hall, where a fire crackled good cheer, and a well-assorted array of hats and coats bespoke a convivial gathering, several loungers were revealed. As the sour man and the pretty girl entered, the unbidden visitor heard the former mention the name of the host, " Major Trefusis."

Captain O'Hagan the maid eyed doubtfully. The new arrival smiled an evil triumph. But O'Hagan calmly handed his card to the girl.

" Request Major Trefusis to step this way ! " he said.

His pose, as, standing just within the hall, he raised his glass and surveyed the guests, was a liberal education in deportment ; his supreme self-possession a pure delight, a thing humanly inimitable.

II.

THE OTHER.

Major Trefusis, retired, with an Indian liver but a warm heart, made a rushing entry, O'Hagan's card in hand.

"What! brought a friend, Repton? Delighted to have you, Captain!"

The sour and wrath-sore Repton raised a protesting hand. His hat and coat the maid had taken charge of; his pretty companion, not daring to dally longer, had escaped into a drawing-room, with a smothered peal of musical laughter.

"One moment, Major!" Mr. Repton drew his sandy eyebrows together and glared upon the intruder. "This fellow is no friend of mine. He imagines that I have offended him and has followed me here, demanding my name and address like a confounded policeman!"

O'Hagan fixed his eyes upon Mr. Repton with quelling glance.

"You have likened me to a confounded

policeman, sir. For which new insult I shall pull your nose!" He turned to Major Trefusis, in that hour the most surprised man from Land's End to John O'Groats. "Mr. Repton is your guest, Major, and of him I shall say nothing, except that he has insulted me; deliberately, and several times. Our cause of misunderstanding is no concern of yours, happily; but as a brother officer and a gentleman you will support my claim to know where I may call upon Mr. Repton to-morrow?"

The Major's prominent, Cambridge eyes regarded the quivering Mr. Repton, whose wrath yet was badly bottled, and escaped in divers sibilant exclamations.

"Don't you know, Repton"—he said; "I mean to say, Repton, the Captain is within his rights, damme if he's not! Why the blazes won't you give him your card—what?"

"Because I don't choose to hand my card to any ruffian who cares to ask for it, Major!"

Thus, Mr. Repton, making an effective exit by the same opening as the lady.

Major Trefusis watched him go, and his red face grew redder, and his wiry moustache more aggressively porcupinish. He snorted, cleared his throat, and turned to O'Hagan—who anticipated him:

"I regret this incident exceedingly, Major. Pray accept my very sincere apologies——"

"Not at all, Captain—not at all! You're the O'Hagan who was with the —th Irish Guards in South Africa—what? Heard of you! heard of you! Delighted to meet you! It's an ill wind—what?"

They shook hands warmly.

"If Repton wasn't my guest—and my sister's guest," continued Major Trefusis, "I'd say he was a puppy and that I'd always thought so! But he's in my house, and I can't tell you what he doesn't want to tell you himself. You're just in time for dinner, Captain!"

"But, Major——"

"Give me your coat, man ——"

"Really, Major——!"

"Brothers in arms and all that, what! Damme! you've *got* to stay!"

"I fear I am intruding——"

"Tut! tut! Come and have a peg. Just time! Were you in Kandahar when ——" etc., etc.

And the pair, arm-in-arm, drifted off together—more strangely met than any two the classic muse has sung. O'Hagan's reluctance in a degree was sincere, for he had formed a strong attachment for the Major at sight and would not gladly have inconvenienced him. But, on the other hand, no human power, save of course physically superior force, could have moved him from that house until his scrupulous honour was satisfied. Had his host proved of a different kidney, then O'Hagan patiently would have patrolled the neighbourhood until the reappearance of his man.

It is recorded, O'Hagan will tell you, that his ancestor Patrick, sometime of the Musketeers of Louis XIII., on one occasion waited for eight hours in the snow outside the hôtel of the Duchesse de C——, in order to reprimand an unknown nobleman who had trodden on his corn. But within eight minutes from the time of the gentleman's coming out, Patrick O'Hagan had aroused the concierge of the Hôtel de C—— to take him in again, summoned a surgeon, summoned a priest, summoned an undertaker, and reported for duty at the Louvre. A bloody ancestor for any man.

My friend's code, then, is peculiar, but iron-bound. He scrupulously avoided the topic of Mr. Repton with his host; but when, later, Mrs. Lestrange, the Major's sister, came in to dinner on the arm of Captain O'Hagan, the countenance of Repton would have served as model for a Notre Dame gargoyle.

The Major, too, had been whispering to one man: "*The* O'Hagan! You recall the incident at so-and-so?" And to another: "O'Hagan, V.C.! One of the O'Hagan's of Dunnamore!" To a girl: "You must have read how the Boers ambushed a company of the So-and-So's at So-and-So? Kipling has written about it! Well, this is Captain O'Hagan, who," etc., etc.

So that, altogether, my friend has assured

me that he recalls no more enjoyable evening. His conversation is always brilliant, but on this occasion, I gather, he surpassed himself. All eyes were fixed upon the handsome, debonair visitant from an older world of romance; for O'Hagan is at heart a Musketeer. Moira Cumberley in particular found him wholly entrancing; and each glance of her bright eyes which rested upon the cavalierly figure, likewise poured gall and wormwood into two souls. One of these souls was the sombre soul of Repton; the other was the joyous but hungry soul of a certain Mr. Bruce McIvor.

("I could see how the wind blew," O'Hagan will explain. "McIvor was the favoured swain, and naturally enough; for he was a fine lad and descended from Robert Bruce. When, later in the evening, I was presented to Mrs. Cumberley—Moira's mother—I discovered the fly in the ointment. Repton had money—but no blood, my boy; no family—and poor McIvor, though he could trace back to Bruce, was a mere free-lance journalist. Mrs. Cumberley also lacked breed, but worshipped Pluto. She had banned the McIvor and encouraged Repton. I saw my course plainly.")

When my friend Bernard O'Hagan sees his course plainly, there are squalls a-brewing for any unhappy wight who queries the Captain's navigation.

III.

NATURAL SELECTION.

Moira sat out a dance with O'Hagan in the conservatory. Needless to say, the Captain does not dance. McIvor's sighful acknowledgment of the girl's disappearance rose above the music. Repton's Mephistophelian glare pierced palm and fern. But Moira blushed, and settled down *tête-à-tête*.

"My dear little girl," said O'Hagan blandly, "you are so very pretty and charming, that I am going to talk to you seriously about your lovers."

Moira gasped as the amazing Captain took her hand and patted it paternally. Without preamble he had placed the conversation upon a thrilling level. It was a unique experience, but she rather liked it.

"Now, I sincerely hope you do not care for Mr. Repton," continued O'Hagan; "because late to-night or early to-morrow morning I propose to pull his nose!"

"Oh!" said Moira. But the language of her eloquent eyes added: "Do him good!"

"He has asked you to marry him?"

(A rebellious glance).

"Has he not?"

(Slight nod).

"You have not yet given him your answer?"

(Head-shake).

"I am glad of that; because I want you to marry Bruce McIvor," explained O'Hagan judicially.

"Indeed!" snapped Moira, with a mutinous shrug of pretty shoulders.

"Yes," said O'Hagan. "I will tell you why. He is a handsome, fine man, and one of a brave and ancient race. He loves you in a way altogether different from Repton's way."

"Has he told you so?"—frigidly.

"No. I have not had an opportunity to speak to him yet! But it is so. With the stimulus of your affection, Moira, with the chance of such a prize as you, he will go far. I understand men of family, my dear, and I tell you that Bruce is a splendid fellow. As for you, Moira, I can only say that I should like to marry you, myself! But since that is impossible, I want it to be Bruce."

He was curiously impersonal; a kind of directing Beneficence which from an Olympic height smoothed the tangled skeins of lesser lives. But there was a finality in his pronouncements against whose thrall the girl fought stubbornly with all the armoury of her woman-soul. For another than Bernard O'Hagan thus to have championed McIvor must have spelled ruin for McIvor's cause; but if O'Hagan had been pressing the suit of an unknown, and not that of one towards whom the girl was predisposed favourably, his advocacy must have told. Moira experienced a sense of weakness; later, of absolute futility.

Once submit to the yoke of O'Hagan's regal patronage, and you are lost. You become a mere pawn. His majestic interference is a stupendous force.

Mr. Repton appeared to claim a dance.

Muffled thunder seemed to be called for and a little incidental music in the form of a sustained chord in G minor.

"I have been having a chat with Moira, sir," said O'Hagan, haughtily, rising as Repton entered.

The muscles of Repton's jaws stood out, lumpish.

"We have decided," continued the cool voice, "that your suit must be withdrawn! It is distasteful to Moira—and distasteful to me!"

Repton's face, in the dimness, showed a greyish white. He swallowed noisily—and took a step towards Captain O'Hagan. Moira clutched at the Captain's arm. She did not fully realise what had happened. Only she knew that this strange man, who half fascinated and half frightened her, had precipitated a climax in her life; had, from no personal motive that she could fathom—unless antipathy from Repton and friendliness to a descendant of Bruce—brought her love affairs violently to a head.

Resentment found place in her heart. Captain O'Hagan was a mere chance acquaintance. Yet—wondrous, expansively human O'Hagan!—she gladly sank her individuality in the overflowing lake of his own and was not philosopher enough to know the source of her contentment. Repton had been very attentive, had spent his money lavishly, but he had been more exacting than his position warranted. What a pity that Bruce was so poor!

For the world (so Moira's mother taught) was ruled by a gilded Providence with a rod of iron; a rod of iron tipped with a magical talisman—a bright new sovereign.

Mr. Repton achieved speech.

"Is it—true . . . what this . . . ruffian . . . says?"

"I note that you call me a ruffian, sir," said O'Hagan icily.

Moira Cumberley was trembling.

"I am—awfully sorry," she answered, speaking with difficulty, "that this—has come about. Don't think I want to be bad friends, Mr. Repton. I want us to be friends always. But——"

"She cannot entertain marriage with a man whose nose I shall pull in the morning!" concluded O'Hagan. "I have other plans for her future. Your card, sir—and you may go!"

Is there another living could have framed such a speech?—another who could have carried such a situation in such a manner? I challenge you to produce him.

Repton turned on his heel. Of words he was bereft again; action was impossible.

IV.

AT FIG TREE COURT.

I.

CAPTAIN O'HAGAN entered my rooms whilst I was at breakfast—hatless, as is his custom; debonair, as he cannot fail to be. His presence has the curious effect of changing relative values. His individuality absorbs: one can no longer describe the scene: the scene is Captain O'Hagan. As he lounges upon the blue Chesterfield, with that odd pose of the hip which suggests that a rapier swings there, I often think that had he flourished contemporaneously with Velasquez he had surely inspired the artist to a supreme achievement. "Portrait of the Chevalier Bernard O'Hagan," must have been counted the Spanish master's *chef d'œuvre*.

"My dear Raymond, are you acquainted with a person of the name of Repton?"

"Sidney Repton, company promoter, newspaper proprietor, and so forth?"

"That will be the fellow! He gave me the slip last night! My position, as a guest, precluded the possibility of obtaining his address from another guest; and the fellow left without his hat. But his address was not in his hat. Where does he live?"

"39A, Fig Tree Court."

"Will you come around with me?"

"For what purpose?"

"I am going to pull his nose!"

"He will probably prosecute you!"

"I think not. But I am entirely at his service. And what about Bruce McIvor?"

"McIvor is a man of great promise. He has been unfortunate. He would make an ideal leader-writer. But he lacks the necessary influence to secure such a post."

O'Hagan frowned thoughtfully.

"He lacks incentive, Raymond," he said. "A man who can trace his ancestry to Robert Bruce requires no influence other than that of blood. Blood, my boy! that is the secret of success! When he is engaged to the girl he loves—the girl I have chosen for him—he will go far. Mark my words, Raymond; he will go far."

"I was unaware that he was a friend of yours."

"I have never spoken to him! But it is unnecessary. A leader-writer, you say? On behalf of an old-established and soundly Conservative organ, of course? Such vacancies, I take it, are rare?"

"Very rare. The leader-writer of the *Universe* is about to become editor. That will create a vacancy. But poor McIvor is not in the running."

"How is that?"

"Well—your friend, Repton, is a big shareholder—managing director. And Repton—for some reason—is no friend to McIvor."

"The reason is evident to me, Raymond. But I am wasting time. I shall be too late to pull Repton's nose; and, owing to other engagements, the pleasure would have to be unduly postponed if I missed him this morning. Are you ready?"

"My dear fellow, you really must excuse me!"

O'Hagan rose, picked up his cane as though it were a sword, swung his shoulders as though to adjust a bandolier, and sighed sadly.

"I am disappointed in you, Raymond. Your ancestor, who helped to hold Limerick, would be disappointed in you, too, I fear. You are tainted with the modern heresies which substitute the solicitor for the second, the divorce-court for the rapier. Good-morning."

The dignified displeasure of the Hon. Bernard O'Hagan is a dire penalty for any man to incur. The Captain retired from my rooms as who should say, "There is a plebeian strain somewhere here!" It was a Charles rebuking a Buckingham; save that the Buckingham was a sorry Villiers, and the Charles a credit to the house of Stuart.

Leaving me to my breakfast and my humiliation, proceed with O'Hagan to No. 39A, Fig Tree Court.

His loud and long ring upon the bell of Repton's chambers brought that monied and harried bachelor in person to the door,

Repton wore slippers and a dressing-gown. His pale, blonde face faded a tone upon recognition of his early caller. Some dread there was, mingled with the anger of a man used to the servility which Talent accords to Capital; for the calmly persistent and imperious truculence of Captain O'Hagan is awesome.

O'Hagan extended his arm and seized Repton's prominent nose in a vice-grip.

Uttering a furious imprecation, Sidney Repton struck out at him. But a pupil of Shashu Myuku (Grand Master of the Higher Jiu-Jitsu) is elusive as a marsh-light. There are not six Europeans, my friend has assured me, initiated in the occultry of Japanese super-force.

Repton's fists met vacancy. Obedient to a power which, seemingly percolating from his nose through every nerve of his body, rendered him helpless—log-like—Repton dropped, panting, to his knees. O'Hagan thrust him prostrate, entered, and closed the door behind him. The feat apparently was performed effortless; such is the outstanding wonder of this science (called, I believe, *judo*).

"Police!" gasped the outraged man. "Help! *Police!*"

"Sir," said O'Hagan sternly, "I should not exploit these arts upon a gentleman. But your whole conduct has shown me plainly that you are not one. However, I shall now resort to the ordinary methods employed to chastise an offensive churl."

He removed a light grey glove (imbrued with the blood of Repton), cast it contemptuously from him; and, as Repton rose, clutching the maltreated organ, O'Hagan grasped his heavy cane with unmistakable intent.

"Now," said O'Hagan, standing on the threshold, "you will recall having referred to me as an 'overdressed puppy'! I have yet to deal with you in regard to the offensive terms 'lunatic,' 'ruffian,' and 'confounded policeman!'"

"Curse you! I'll kill you!" panted Repton, and crouched, looking up to O'Hagan with glaring, malignant eyes which, at that moment indeed, mirrored a murderous soul.

"I think not," was the reply. "Others have attempted the feat; but I am here to-day, alive to resent insult."

The other did not rise. Repton already was defeated. The business-like ferocity of O'Hagan, the absolute efficiency of his methods, caused to evaporate what remained of the quality vaguely labelled Courage, leaving only the brine of bitter anger and mortification.

"What do you want?" he said slowly, racking his muddled brains for a mode of retribution which should not render him ridiculous.

He stood up and backed toward his desk.

"Remain where you are!" directed O'Hagan, pointing his cane. "Attempt to reach any weapon, and I shall thrash you until I am tired!"

"I am unarmed," muttered Repton sullenly. "You have a heavy stick."

The situation was wildly bizarre—unlike anything within his experience; of which he had dreamed. The querulous voice did not seem his own.

O'Hagan placed his cane upon a chair, and raised the monocle.

"Do you contemplate an attack?" he asked, with a kind of pleased surprise.

Repton dropped into an armchair, and sank his face in his hands. His inflamed nose robbed the scene of a certain pathos which otherwise had found place there.

"You will sit at your desk," said O'Hagan, "and write a note to the new editor of the *Universe* informing him that Mr. Bruce McIvor will be his leader-writer."

Repton was galvanised. He started up; clutched the chair-arms.

"I shall not! Your damned interference in my affairs——" His voice broke.

"Very well." O'Hagan took up his cane. "The alternative is equally pleasing to me."

"Look here!" Repton was on his feet again, hands twitching. "I've got no chance with you! You're a bully!——"

"I warn you that I regard those words as a new insult. Indeed, that is the greatest insult of all. Should you term one a bully who sued you for slander?" O'Hagan's eyes were bright. "Learn, that when you insult a gentleman, the choice of weapons is his! The law is a weapon for those who cannot fight their own battles, not for such as I!"

Ah! what would you have given to have heard him deliver that speech? But you cannot even picture him, head aloft, foot advanced; hear the ringing voice; quail before the flashing eye.

Repton wrote.

"Now, a letter to McIvor, giving him the appointment at the same salary as his predecessor."

Repton grasped at the desk. The ferrule of O'Hagan's cane tapped upon the writing-pad.

"At the same salary as his predecessor, Mr. Repton."

The note was written.

"Ring up all your fellow-directors, or all whom you can," ordered the Captain, "and tell them of this appointment."

Repton hesitated. To comply was to burn

his boats. The cane quivered in O'Hagan's nervous grasp.

"It's irregular. It may be annulled at Wednesday's meeting."

"If it is annulled I shall thrash you in public, when and where I next meet you. You will be at liberty to take what steps you please."

Lifting the receiver from the hook, Sidney Repton made several calls, briefly communicating to those who ruled the *Universe* that Mr. Bruce McIvor was a desirable acquisition to the literary staff. He was vanquished. In aught save exact compliance he saw ridicule—the contempt of Fleet Street.

He turned to O'Hagan, pale faced, eyes flaming. Words trembled unspoken upon his tongue.

"Stop!"

O'Hagan spoke the word imperiously, and raised his hand.

"You have bought immunity," he continued, "in respect of your insults from 'overdressed puppy' to 'bully.' Any you may utter henceforward I shall deal with separately."

He strode toward the door; turned in a flash . . . and struck a revolver out of Repton's hand. Stooping, he picked it from the carpet.

"I shall consider my action in the matter of this murderous assault, Mr. Repton," he said icily. "My behaviour will largely depend upon your own."

He slipped the weapon into his pocket, and turned again. The door slammed behind him.

II.

We caught Bruce McIvor just as he was about to go out. I think I have never seen a man quite so blankly amazed as he when the letter of appointment was placed in his hand. I am more or less accustomed to the various emotions expressed by the victims of O'Hagan's extraordinary philanthropy;

but McIvor was positively alarming. He seemed to be dazed.

I think he experienced that kind of sentiment which makes a Frenchman weep, intoxicates an Irishman, but chokes a Scotsman.

In the cab which O'Hagan had in waiting we were a silent trio. O'Hagan leant back humming a gay melody, whilst McIvor sat watching him as if he half expected him to vanish like some Arabian *ginn*.

Into a charming little villa we filed. McIvor's nervousness was appalling. He kept close to my distinguished friend, and hung upon his words as though in them alone he hoped for salvation. In a pretty, *petite* drawing-room we waited; the young Scot, seated on the edge of a chair, looking like a man on trial for murder; I hard put to it to preserve a serene countenance; and O'Hagan wandering from picture to picture, and surveying each through his uplifted monocle with the critical gaze of a connoisseur.

Then he turned the glass upon the door, drawing himself up with inimitable grandeur

Entered a very pretty girl, and a very prim lady, more mature; excellently but dryly, preserved.

McIvor rose and coughed and looked everywhere but straight before him. The pretty girl blushed frantically. The other lady stared, extending her hand to O'Hagan.

O'Hagan bowed. O'Hagan's bow is a notable event.

His neat introductory speech ended with something to the effect that—

"My friend, Mr. Lawrence Raymond, would like to be counted among *your* friends."

I was acknowledged.

"I am delighted, Miss Cumberley," he continued, linking his arm in that of McIvor and drawing him forward, "to present to you the new leader-writer of the *Universe.* Mrs. Cumberley—your future son-in-law. Congratulations!"

Can you picture the scene? I think not. Heavens! what a man! I take off my hat to Bernard O'Hagan.

EXPLOIT THE THIRD.
HE MEETS THE LEOPARD LADY.

EXPLOIT THE THIRD.

HE MEETS THE LEOPARD LADY.

I.

THE BOOM-MAKER.

My friend Captain O'Hagan frequently is misunderstood; his studied singularity of appearance is falsely ascribed to a desire for notoriety. Whereas he eschews and abominates publicity of any kind, and merely seeks to establish a visible distinction betwixt the aristocrat and the plebeian.

The ever-increasing facilities for airing one's grievances in long primer, he contends, are destructive of that chaste reserve once characteristic of our race. I agree with O'Hagan. He declares that we love to be interviewed.

"Is it not true, Raymond," he cries, "that for the sake of seeing her photograph (retouched) in the columns of a daily paper, Mrs. Brown-Jones will reveal to the blushing public the secret of her corsets? Does she not draw attention to the graceful contour of her form, and she (the mother of a family) take the man in the street into her confidence, imparting to him intimate particulars respecting her wardrobe which, if used indiscreetly, would prove most compromising?"

"Alas, O'Hagan," I reply, "it is so."

He throws himself back in his chair, purple-lined cloak widely flying; picturesque, hatless head raised in scorn. He is the focus of a hundred gazes.

"A young lady," he continues, "whom one might assume from her picture in the advertisement column to be not wholly destitute of modesty, will inform edified readers that 'until Mrs. Hodge brought me a box of Nippo Ointment my face was one red mass of pimples!' She will declare that formerly she was unable to sleep at night owing to the itching of her back!"

HE MEETS THE LEOPARD LADY

His scorn is terrible; superbly fearful. Advertisement is anathema.

We are seated in the Park, wherein at the moment no one else is talked of but my distinguished friend. Those who have the honour of his acquaintance acquire a new popularity with the less fortunate. Several countesses and a charming duchess have repassed us no fewer than nine times. But O'Hagan, serenely insensible to the admiration which he excites in so many bosoms, lounges regally aloof, as one upon a lofty minaret who scarce glances down to the throngs beneath him.

An author of "costume" romances passes. His studiously cultivated resemblance to Napoleon III. usually earns him a buzz of acknowledgment. This morning he moves amid the chill of unrecognition, and raises his prominent moustache fiercely and rudely as he glares at my companion, who usurps all homage.

"That fellow stares in an unwarrantable manner," says O'Hagan; and taking my arm, he proceeds in the same direction.

We overtake the author, despite my lagging footsteps; for I perceive that my friend is bent upon some extravagant act.

"Pardon me, sir!"

The author turns, glaring.

"But are you connected with the house of Buonaparte?"

The author, puzzled, faintly gratified:

"Not directly, sir. But what——"

"I regret that, sir. I cherish an antipathy from the family which I may term hereditary. Your reply deprives me of the pleasure of trimming your *mustachios!*"

The man is stricken speechless. It is such an encounter as he has portrayed (on paper) a score of times. But in the actuality it finds him lacking.

"For your whole appearance is most distasteful to me," concludes the Captain. "Good morning."

(We proceed.)

A trembling voice which says something about "a letter from my solicitor," reaches our ears, faintly.

HE MEETS THE LEOPARD LADY 91

"The solicitor again, Raymond!" laughs O'Hagan. "Never the friend to measure the length of one's blade! Your knights of the pen make sorry cavaliers!"

I grant it. And the worst of my bad dreams is that wherein—unaccompanied by the magnificent and terrible O'Hagan—I encounter some of those whom he has browbeaten in my presence!

But, as I think I already have stated, O'Hagan sometimes is misunderstood.

At a certain club, of which O'Hagan is not a member, my friend was introduced to an American gentleman who proclaimed himself a press agent.

("I like Americans—real, full-blooded, whole-hearted Americans," O'Hagan has told me. "I can even appreciate how, in an American, commercial acumen and gentility may be wedded. My great granduncle, Edmond, distinguished himself, as you remember, in the Civil War."

His great grand-uncle, Edmond, is a favourite source of anecdote; but the impression left upon my mind is that a more truculent, bloodthirsty swashbuckler never breathed God's air.)

"I am very delighted to have met you, Captain O'Hagan," said the press agent, whose name was Alex. Dewson. "I would like to put up a proposition right now!"

O'Hagan fumbled, impressively, for the broad black ribbon upon which depends his monocle. He raised the glass, and, holding it at some little distance from his right eye, surveyed the speaker. O'Hagan's right eye, magnified by the pebble, can show, on occasions, as a large grey orb of intolerance.

"You interest me, Mr. Dewson."

"I'll interest you some more yet, sir!" declared Dewson, with cheery confidence. "It's likely you'll have heard of a little author called Ronald Brandon?"

He spoke the words waggishly; as one might say: "You may have heard a little Stratford fellow, called Shakespeare, mentioned?"—or, "You've perhaps seen the name of a rather likely figure painter, known as Michelangelo?"

In point of fact, Ronald Brandon really

HE MEETS THE LEOPARD LADY

was a " little " author ; and, as it happened, O'Hagan never had heard of him. He has never heard of *any* modern fictionists ; he regards them *all* with immeasurable contempt. Mr. Dewson's question was purely a rhetoric question, however, and he proceeded without pausing for a reply :

"His new book (it'll break all the windows) is ' Jules Sanquin, Duellist.' He's placed his press work in my hands, and I've been looking for an introduction to you, Captain, for over a week ! I can put up a proposition to net you a pile ! "

" Indeed ! " said O'Hagan, icily.

(" Such people as Dewson," he has confided to me, " are calculated to bring disgrace upon a national character. He was the type of man who would have sought an audience with His Holiness the Pope, and ' put up a proposition ' to boom St. Peter's.")

" My client, as you'll know," continued the irrepressible press agent, " is top-hole as a swordsman. Took out the team a year ago that beat the Frenchmen."

Captain O'Hagan stared.

"They tell me *you're* pretty handy," resumed Dewson; " so here's the goods in a nutshell: I'll send down a shorthand-typist to your chambers to take a few notes; put a sound man to work; and in a week or a fortnight ' My Affaires of Honour and Gallantry, by Captain the Hon. Bernard O'Hagan,' will be in the press! I can promise you an *advance* of £500, my dear sir! Meanwhile, you insult Brandon, and meet him with rapiers on the French coast—press, cinema men, etc., in attendance. Out comes ' Jules Sanquin, Duellist '—five editions subscribed! Out comes ' My Affaires of Honour and Gallantry '—libraries gasping! How d'you like the title? *Affaires*—see? French. Get the literary flavour right on the cover! How d'you like the proposition?"

The intolerant grey eye scrutinised the brogues upon Mr. Dewson's feet and rose by gradations to the Stetson felt adorning the apex of his commercial brain.

"Is this delightful scheme a child of your own fecundity, Mr. Dewson, or has Mr. Ronald Brandon any share in its parentage?"

HE MEETS THE LEOPARD LADY 95

"I'm out raising no man's laurel wreaths," declared Dewson. "The proposition's Brandon's. How does it appeal to you?"

"That portion of the 'proposition,'" said O'Hagan, with frigid courtesy, "which has reference to a meeting on the French coast appeals to me keenly!"

II.

LA BELLE LOTUS.

Those of you who have the privilege to be acquainted with my friend Bernard O'Hagan will find much scope for wonderment in the circumstance that Mr. Dewson proceeded thus far and survived, intact. No one but a successful press agent could possibly have mistaken the significance of the Captain's icy calm. Anyone who, knowing him, had adventured upon such a proposal, must have been aware that, so doing, he carried his life in his hand. Mr. Dewson remained placidly ignorant of the fires which he was coaling.

"Will you come along now to Brandon's flat?" he suggested, in his brisk way.

"It will afford me great pleasure. I am most anxious to meet Mr. Brandon!"

Passing over the short journey, then—throughout which almost every word of Mr. Dewson's inspired O'Hagan with a new wonder at the shamelessness of the times, and added fuel to his resentment—enter the house of Ronald Brandon, novelist.

"Here he is, Brandon!" cried the press agent. "He's coming in on it!"

Ronald Brandon was a tall and good-looking young man, carrying a certain athletic arrogance with poor grace. From his perfectly groomed fair hair to his white spatted, immaculately glossy boots he was an incarnate error of judgment. He had been encouraged to think himself a celebrity—and the whole thing was a mistake. He was not even in the same flight with the double of Napoleon III.

HE MEETS THE LEOPARD LADY 97

His casually extended hand Captain O'Hagan failed to observe. O'Hagan bowed with exceeding fine formality.

"Going to have a little bout with me, Captain?" laughed Brandon lightly.

"I am looking forward to it," was the reply, "provided your status admits of my crossing swords with you."

Dewson and Brandon stared uncomprehendingly.

"I mean, are you of gentle blood? To what Brandons do you belong?"

The novelist continued to stare.

"My governor is James Brandon, K.C., if that's what you're driving at!"

"Professional people?" said O'Hagan with exquisite condescension. "Never mind. For our present purpose, sufficiently respectable."

What the now incensed Brandon might have said to that will never be known, for he was interrupted by the ringing of the bell, by the almost immediate entrance of a loudly pretty woman who was furiously overdressed, who struck the vision a sharp blow, from which one's outraged eyes blinkingly recoiled. She was arrayed in a long coat of leopard's skin, wore a motor bonnet of the same material, from the left side whereof, rearward, swept a golden plume of incredible length. Her hair was of the hue sometimes called Titian, but would have made Titian weep blood.

This lady—who proved to be French—was introduced as La Belle Lotus.

"Another client of mine, Captain!" explained Dewson, affably anxious to dissipate the thundery atmosphere which had settled upon the establishment. Brandon was scowling ferociously. "She is the latest sensation in dancers, sir. Her 'Dance of Delilah' is the talk of London! This is the lady you'll quarrel about. Savvy? Three birds with one stone! All town will rush to see the girl two big men have fought over. Up go her bookings! How's that for a three-handed boost? The limit?"

O'Hagan raised his glass.

"It strikes me as being appreciably beyond the limit!" he drawled. "But what has

HE MEETS THE LEOPARD LADY

led you to suppose that I am desirous of publishing my memoirs?"

"You're not out throwing away thousands, I take it?"

"On the contrary, Mr. Dewson. But, emphatically, I shall not publish any kind of book. You may omit that item from your 'proposition.'"

La Belle surveyed the speaker appreciatively. Brandon watched him in angry perplexity. Dewson's round eyes grew rounder.

"You don't mean to say——"

"I have no intention of disturbing your admirable arrangements, Mr. Dewson. You may rely upon me to meet Mr. Brandon."

"But 'My Affaires'"——

"Dismiss the idea. It is out of the question."

"Then what are you doing it for?"

O'Hagan, having examined minutely the visible attractions of La Belle Lotus—so minutely as to make her blush—dropped his glass.

"Your proposal is of such a nature,

sir," he replied calmly, "that no gentleman could decline to accept it."

"I want to know how we stand," burst in Brandon, his choler enhanced by the evident inability of the lady to withstand O'Hagan's frank gaze. "Are you——"

"Am I going to meet you on the French coast, sir?" O'Hagan anticipated. "Emphatically, yes! Rely upon me!"

"That's good," rapped Dewson. "We'll talk about the book, later. When you see eye to eye with me you won't want to drop it. But you're game for the little passage of arms? That's the talk! Well, talking's dry work. What about——"

"Excuse me." O'Hagan raised his hand. "Pray excuse me!"

"But we've made no arrangements."

"I am listening, Mr. Dewson."

Dewson felt that he was being hustled.

"Well, I'd planned it to start on Wednesday night. Brandon and Yvette—La Belle—are having supper at Varano's. I'm there, too; but not at the same table. Press boys there, of course. You blow in, and say or do

HE MEETS THE LEOPARD LADY

something which Brandon's supposed to take as an insult."

O'Hagan, his head attentively tilted, nodded. La Belle was watching him, now, fascinatedly.

"I shall observe your wishes implicitly, Mr. Dewson!"

"Bit of a scene. Cards exchanged. Pars in the press."

"A proviso, sir. My name shall not be mentioned."

"Not mentioned!"

"Let all the credit be Mr. Brandon's. I remain anonymous."

"It's sure to come out later. I don't understand——"

"I am aware of that, Mr. Dewson! On the following morning, if I do not mistake you, Mr. Brandon's friends call upon me, and the meeting is arranged?"

"That's it! We're supposed to be hushing it up, see? But it kind of leaks out!"

"Precisely. At what hour will Mr. Brandon be supping?"

"Say half-past eleven."

"It is an appointment."

Captain O'Hagan bowed to the leopard lady, looking challengingly into her eyes—turned from Messrs. Brandon and Dewson, and walked to the door. Upon Brandon's tongue unutterable things trembled. Mr. Dewson was not entirely at his ease.

III.

THE BOOM.

Captain O'Hagan entered Varano's at half-past eleven on Wednesday evening. No more need be said. A sensation amongst the guests is understood.

For a moment he paused, glass raised. His pose was a poem in grace; his mode of surveying those who supped was a tribute so deliciously keen as almost to be insulting. He focussed the table whereat Ronald

HE MEETS THE LEOPARD LADY 103

Brandon and the dancer were seated. Amid a cathedral silence, impressive and oppressive, he traversed the supper-room. To say that he crossed it would be inaccurate and inadequate; he traversed it.

"Sir!"—he bent over Brandon—"one moment. Mademoiselle!"—he smiled upon La Belle Yvette—"might I entreat you to step aside with me?"

She glanced at Brandon, flushing with excitement now that the moment of the "boom" was come. Brandon, who vainly had besought Dewson to recast the comedy—omitting O'Hagan—examined his finger nails. He was acting poorly. In fact he was pronouncedly "fluffy."

La Belle rose and stepped aside with O'Hagan. She wore an amazingly daring and dazzlingly brilliant evening toilette; a tight-fitting silk gown coloured in imitation of a leopard's skin. Dewson identified his clients with certain "make-ups" or trademarks. Thus, La Belle Lotus was "the leopard lady."

Imagine every eye in Varano's supper-room

to be centred upon this wildly picturesque pair. O'Hagan, his cloak cast back in purple splendour, rested one hand upon his hip with a gesture which had not been inconsistent with the act of depressing a rapier hilt.

"Are you quite sure"— he bent towards her with inimitable gallantry—"that a scene here will enhance your professional reputation?"

She glanced up rapidly—and down again, shyly. She could not recall having feared to meet any man's eye prior to encountering Captain O'Hagan.

"Mr. Dewson—he says so; and Mr. Dewson is so clever. He never makes mistakes."

"I concede that Mr. Dewson is clever; but nevertheless he makes mistakes, mademoiselle. I am impartial. I can insult Mr. Brandon without involving you in any way. But, if you wish to be involved, command me."

La Belle felt singularly helpless. Instinctively she divined that the forceful Mr.

HE MEETS THE LEOPARD LADY

Dewson and the imperious Captain O'Hagan were advancing to no common end.

"It is better that we keep to Mr. Dewson's arrangements, I think."

"Very well."

O'Hagan proffered his arm. He led her doorward. A sibilant chorus of gasps arose. Brandon was up, now. His face flushed deeply, and paled, vying in its pallor with the serviette which he crushed in one shaking hand. He thrust back his chair.

A staccato cough drew his gaze to a distant table. Mr. Dewson—conscientious stage-manager—feared that one of the cast was like to overact his rôle. Brandon hesitated, fuming.

La Belle Yvette knew a fearful joy. Her inordinate vanity was gratified by this scene, but even her great daring recoiled from that which pended. Yet she offered no real resistance. True, she placed her hand upon O'Hagan's, but he calmly clasped it in his own.

"Act as I direct," he said, bending his picturesque head and looking into the half-fearful eyes.

He glanced aside to where the head-waiter stood, a figure of pitiable indecision, a study in fatuous ineptitude.

"My man—this lady's cloak."

Upon the hushed silence of the supper-room the words rang out sharply.

The head-waiter hesitated. The head-waiter at Varano's is a person of proper proportions and seemly dignity. It is no part of his important functions menially to run for hats and cloaks. O'Hagan's unoccupied hand raised the glass.

"Were you aware that I gave you an order?"

The head-waiter became aware of the awesome fact. He departed.

Brandon's chair fell backward. A wineglass was dropped with a crash upon the floor beside Mr. Dewson's table. But the prompting of the ingenious press agent now was unheeded. The novelist strode down the room. One or two of the male visitors half rose. Some of the women began to look frightened.

"Damn your impudence! Release that lady!"

HE MEETS THE LEOPARD LADY 107

Dewson slipped from his place and joined the interesting group. He placed his hand warningly upon Brandon's shoulder.

"Don't lose your wool!" he whispered. "It's going great!"

Brandon shook him off.

"Do you hear me? Release that lady! Yvette! stand aside, I beg of you! I have something to say to this person!"

La Belle looked from face to face. All was not well here. Only Captain O'Hagan seemed at ease: he should be the star of her guidance!

The head-waiter returning, the Captain assisted mademoiselle to endue her leopard-skin cloak.

Brandon's fists clenched and re-opened convulsively.

"Yvette!" He almost choked. "You are not going *away*?—not going to leave me here—a laughing stock——"

"Mr. Ronald Brandon!" O'Hagan placed his arm protectingly about mademoiselle's shoulders and stared through the monocle at the novelist's pale face. "I do not approve of this lady's being in your company!"

Brandon fell back (O'Hagan's divine audacity can strike as a physical blow) into the arms of Mr. Dewson.

"Stick to your part!" hissed the latter in his ear; and held him firmly. "This is a treat! All the restaurant heard what he said! Heard your name, too!"

"Curse you! Let go!"

The veins swelled upon Brandon's forehead; his eyes protruded.

Captain O'Hagan, serenely:

"Come, mademoiselle! This vulgar brawler is no fit companion for us!"

Half the guests were upon their feet now. Someone had gone for the manager. The horror-frozen head-waiter met the Gorgon gaze which hypnotically sought him through the pebble. He turned and swung wide the door.

Brandon made a savage leap. Dewson grabbed his coat tails.

Mademoiselle, trembling slightly, having

quitted the room, O'Hagan turned, and tossed his card at Brandon's feet.

"You may care further to discuss the matter at some future time," he said coldly. "I am otherwise engaged this evening!"

Brandon broke loose at that, but collided with the head-waiter, who began to feel faint. A tremendous buzz of conversation arose. Above it sounded the shrill note of a whistle. O'Hagan, without, had ordered a taxi. Then someone laughed—a pressman there for the "story."

The novelist whisked around upon the detaining Mr. Dewson.

"Curse you and your 'boosts'!" he snarled. "You've made me the laughing-stock of London! I'll kill that damned O'Hagan!"

"Good business!" said the press agent. "Do it. Double our sales!"

IV.

ECHOES OF THE BOOM.

O'HAGAN called upon me. His entrances possess electric properties. One's schemes melt; O'Hagan becomes the scheme of all things terrestrial. The future shrinks, bounded by O'Hagan. The universe is "a universe after Captain the Hon. Bernard O'Hagan." An unexpected call by the Tsar of all the Russias could not be more exciting, and one would be less impressed if the Mikado dropped in for a pipe and a Scotch-and-soda.

"I have selected you, Raymond"—he toyed with his monocle—"to act for me in a little affair on the French coast. You will be associated with Lieutenant the Chevalier Camille d'Oysans."

That was bad hearing.

The Chevalier, according to O'Hagan, is "the last of the *grand seigneurs*." I think O'Hagan may be right; and trust he is. This fire-eating Frenchman in my opinion

HE MEETS THE LEOPARD LADY 111

constitutes a menace to society. He would any day rather cut a man's throat than shake hands with him.

(His recent decoration for having personally dispatched a larger number of Boches than any other man in the armies of France, will be a memory fresh in my reader's mind.)

"And I do not expect you to withdraw, Raymond,"—coldly.

Since, on more than one recent occasion, I had been so unfortunate as to incur O'Hagan's displeasure, I perceived that a path was cut for my feet—a path of peril, from which, nevertheless, I might not stray. I understand that Charles II., when it pleased him, could be a king indeed. The fact that O'Hagan inherits a similar capacity from someone or another is not necessarily destructive of what posthumous reputation remains to the lady of his race who ornamented the Stuart court.

He passed to me a press cutting. The paragraph related how an anonymous gentleman had had a public misunderstanding with Mr. Ronald Brandon, the famous author, whose forthcoming work, etc., etc. The misunderstanding had been due to the presence of La Belle Yvette Lotus, the beautiful dancer, etc., etc.

"D'Oysans has already arranged the preliminaries," explained O'Hagan. "So all that you have to do, my boy, is to meet me at Victoria to-night at ten-thirty."

"This is incredible!"

"Not at all."

"We shall all stand to be arrested!"

"Never fear. These little affairs are better managed in France!"

"For heaven's sake, what weapons?"

"Swords!"

"In what way are you interested in this girl?"

"In no way. Not in the slightest."

O'Hagan stood up and gracefully executed the Grand Salute with his cane.

"I badly need a little practice," he said. "That is all, Raymond!"

"This man, Ronald Brandon, has some reputation as a swordsman."

"So I hear," replied O'Hagan languidly.

"He has grossly insulted me; so that I am quite looking forward to meeting him. Although he merely comes of a race of attorneys, he appears to have a fine reach."

He yawned slightly. There came a ringing of my door bell, which I proceeded to investigate.

"Might I inquire who the blazes your distinguished visitor is?"

Thus O'Hagan, critically examining a very large size in formidable ruffians who had forced his way past me into the study.

"Which of you is O'Hagan?" demanded the caller, truculently.

He was a man fully six feet two in his boots; wore a peculiarly racy tweed suit, cut morning-coat fashion; a pink soft collar, and a green tie adorned with a big diamond. He was bullet-headed, close shaven, and rejoiced in a prominent jaw of marine blue. He threw a soft hat into a corner and addressed a ferocious glare to each of us in turn.

"You have a broken nose," said the Captain, with icy distaste.

"That's done it! You're 'im!" proclaimed the visitor. "An' you'll 'ave a broken neck in 'alf a mo!"

He stripped off his coat and hurled it amongst the litter of my writing-table. He removed the diamond and placed it in his waistcoat pocket. He tore his collar from his ox-like neck and cast it on the carpet. He began to unbutton his vest.

"This is not a public bath," said O'Hagan, observing these manœuvres through his monocle. "You can have a wash for twopence at the lower end of Langham Place."

The other proceeded stolidly with his immodest toilet, divesting himself of his waistcoat and rolling up his sleeves over his hirsute, brawny arms. No reply he made; he was a man too full for words.

O'Hagan rose from the Chesterfield which is his favourite lounge and stretched himself languidly. He poked the fire and left the poker between the bars.

"Raymond," he drawled, "shall I go and find a constable to throw this low dog down stairs?"

The man leapt to the door with extraordinary agility, locked it, and slipped the key into a back pocket of his trousers. He faced us, a formidable figure, stripped to the pink shirt, which revealed the enormous development of his pectoral muscles. O'Hagan moves amid singular proceedings.

"Now, my bonny gentleman! My name's 'Trooper' Belcher—an' I'm 'er husband!"

"I trust you refer to Mrs. Belcher?"—O'Hagan.

Belcher: "My wife's La Belle Lotus!"

The Captain studied Mr. Belcher with a new curiosity.

"I gather that you are a music-hall pugilist. Am I also to conclude that you are a bully acting on behalf of Mr. Brandon, whom I have to meet at seven in the morning outside Calais?"

"*I* met Mr. bloomin' Brandon at seven this evenin' outside Oxford Circus!" shouted Belcher. "*You'll* meet 'im in Middlesex 'Ospital!"

My wits had deserted me. From the moment that the man had thrust his way into my rooms up to that when he had thus proclaimed himself the assailant of Brandon, I had stood helplessly watching his outrageous proceedings.

("A gentleman, to-day," O'Hagan has informed me, "is utterly at the mercy of the first lusty ruffian who cares to attack him. The only offensive and defensive art which survives to any extent — brutal pugilism — is extensively practised among the lower classes. Where is the gentleman's sword? Taken from him! The Higher Jiu-Jitsu, my dear Raymond, or Art of Gentle Thought, should be included in the curriculum of every preparatory establishment.")

Belcher executed a charge which, I think, would have swept a healthy bullock from its feet. O'Hagan, with a lightning rapidity of action apparently peculiar to pupils of Shashu Myuku of Nagasaki, secured and presented the poker.

The man touched it with one huge fist and recoiled, screaming hoarsely.

"By God! that's 'ot!" he panted.

"It is," replied O'Hagan, again thrusting

HE MEETS THE LEOPARD LADY

the point amid the coals; "red hot!" With his left hand he waved his monocle in my direction. "One cannot soil one's hands with the persons of low fellows, Raymond!"

Belcher snatched up a heavy chair as though it had had no greater weight than a matchbox. A lightning, rapier lunge with the poker—an unpleasant *sizzling* sound—and the chair crashed harmlessly to the floor. The now painfully singed "trooper" fell back on to the Chesterfield, groaning.

Again my bell rang.

"Hand the key to Mr. Raymond, my man," ordered O'Hagan; "and replace your filthy rags upon your indecently nude person."

Belcher threw the key across the carpet. My mind had assimilated a profound truth of the Higher Jiu-Jitsu: brute courage falters in the presence of hot pokers. I went to the door, and upon the landing stood a dazzling vision in leopard skins.

"My 'usband!" (The vision had a French accent.) "Is he here? Yes? Quick!"

She slipped past me, as an animal growl sounded from within. My rooms no longer were my own, but were become a rendezvous for insane meetings—for nightmare encounters. I re-entered the bear-garden which I had been wont to call my study.

The leopard lady was kneeling beside the wounded Mr. Belcher and explaining in voluble syncopated English that his suspicions were groundless, that it was a " boom," no more; that he must *not* kill Captain O'Hagan.

" My impression, Raymond," said the latter, focussing me across the room, " is that our friend Belcher has recently left jail."

" What if I 'ave ! " roared that maltreated ruffian, starting to his feet.

" This," replied O'Hagan with suppressed ferocity, " that if you are present in another minute I shall send you back again ! *Madame !* "—he bowed to La Belle—" kindly remove your property from my friend's apartment—I would suggest that you deposit it in cold storage—and permit me to say that I had credited you with nicer taste!"

He placed a cigarette between his lips, igniting it with the now white-hot poker.

V.

BELCHER THE THOROUGH.

"It is singularly illustrative of the obscure psychology of the lower orders," said Bernard O'Hagan, "this marrying habit of Continental music-hall artistes. The female of the species may drive, take supper, and accept diamonds from men of pedigree; but she always marries a prize-fighter or a bookmaker. It is a process of natural selection, Raymond. When out of the proceeds of a successful professional career she invests in a husband, she 'backs her fancy.' I have known Spanish dancers who were adored by reigning monarchs to have unsavoury husbands concealed in all sorts of filthy alleys; and one lady circus rider to whom I was presented in Budapest proved to be lawfully wedded to a retired Paris sewerman. Zoologically, the habit has interest."

Our inquiries at the hospital discovered Mr. Brandon to be on the danger list.

"The most promising meeting since I encountered Baron Verneux," murmured O'Hagan, "indefinitely postponed! The Chevalier Camille d'Oysans will be keenly disappointed. He had made all the necessary arrangements for flying the country!"

We learned that the police were in quest of Mr. Brandon's assailant. A call at Mr. Alex. Dewson's hotel provided a surprise.

"I shall not chastise him," explained my friend. "The depths of his ignorance are pathetic. But I feel it to be my duty to tell him that he is a disgrace to the great nation which includes in its roll of honour the name of Edmond O'Hagan."

Mr. Dewson could receive no visitors. Captain O'Hagan swept the servant aside and waved to me to follow. It needs some-

HE MEETS THE LEOPARD LADY

thing more than a verbal rebuff to exclude O'Hagan—something in the nature of a double-barred iron door or a squad with fixed bayonets.

My friend honoured Mr. Dewson's apartment. And Mr. Dewson, a heavily bandaged figure hunched up in an arm-chair by the fire, observed our intrusion with his one visible eye.

"Raymond," said O'Hagan, as he focussed this crippled apparition, "the 'Trooper' has forestalled us again!"

"You bet he has, Captain!" whispered a weak voice.

O'Hagan turned to me.

"In the thoroughness of Mr. Belcher's method," he said, "I find something almost admirable, Raymond! The 'Trooper' is a loss to the service."

That he was a loss which speeding Time should rectify, we, being but human, could not foresee. But is it not history how Sergeant Belcher, at a spot not a hundred miles from Ypres, acquired the most coveted distinction in the gift of His Britannic Majesty for rescuing a badly wounded officer under heavy fire? And is it not written in deathless annals that the name of that gallant officer was Captain the Hon. Bernard O'Hagan, V.C., D.S.O.?

EXPLOIT THE FOURTH.
HE BURIES AN OLD LOVE.

EXPLOIT THE FOURTH.

HE BURIES AN OLD LOVE.

I.

THE LONELY LADY.

THAT class distinctions are invidious, that one man is as good as another, are theorems which find no place in O'Hagan's philosophy. His whole life is a protest against such propositions. He complains that there is no badge peculiar to the gentleman; that the latest morning-coat from Savile Row is colourably imitated, and within a week, by Rye Lane, Peckham. Hence, I take it, his broad, black ribbon with the dependent monocle, his purple-lined cloak.

These things are not imitated, and for a simple reason. O'Hagan's cloak makes no appeal to Peckham, and leaves even Hampstead cold.

O'Hagan holds that to tolerate scurrility from the lower classes is to encourage rebellion, and maintains that the French Revolution was brought about, not by the vices of the nobility, but by its weakness.

"Spare the axe and spoil the people," he says.

Upon the necessity for a sort of patrician purple, distinctive of the gentleman, he is insistent, and the episode illustrative of this which he is fond of citing is that of the lonely lady of the Strand.

Captain O'Hagan, then, one evening, was swinging westward along that thoroughfare, hatless, as usual, in evening dress, with his purple-lined cloak flying. Idle curiosity induced him to stroll down that narrow, sloping way which terminates in dungeonesque darkness and arches, but which leads one to the stage door of the Novelty Theatre. At the end of the passage upon which the stage door opens there may sometimes be found sundry loafers. The inexperienced

HE BURIES AN OLD LOVE 127

might assume these to be connected with the Novelty establishment, but would err in so doing. They are connected with a much older establishment; the ancient order of Mouchers.

As O'Hagan came abreast of this place, the sole representative of the ancient order on duty that evening, with a headshake, an upward and a downward glance, and an evil smile, dismissed the inquiry of a young lady who, timidly, had addressed him, and hastened to meet a party of three American comedians as they descended from their car.

The lady, who was quite young, and simply dressed in a dark walking habit, flushed with mortification, and then became very pale as she turned away.

O'Hagan's blood boiled within his veins. It is such a simple, everyday incident as this which renders him really terrible. He hastened after the lady, who was walking slowly in the direction of Charing Cross, and touched her gently upon the arm.

" Madame—your pardon ! "

She turned, startled.

"That fellow at the stage-door was rude to you. I beg, as a favour, that you will grant me permission to reprimand him."

The lady, unmistakably, was displeased. She was dark, and, as O'Hagan observed with æsthetic appreciation, of a delicately aristocratic beauty.

"You are mistaken. Pray do not trouble."

("How," O'Hagan will ask, "could she be expected to know that a stranger addressing her in the Strand was one in whose discretion she might safely confide? To permit any boor to endue a dress suit is to kill chivalry.")

"Madame, I beg that you will not misjudge me. I am not mistaken, neither in my surmise nor as to my plain duty. I do not know your name, nor seek to learn it. Mine is Captain O'Hagan. And had you been a flower-seller I should as staunchly have disputed my right to protect you from insult as I do knowing you to be of my own rank."

HE BURIES AN OLD LOVE 129

She was bewildered. My friend is essentially bewildering. He is not a person whom any man or any woman can hope to snub— to overlook. He comes into one's life, a tangible proposition, which cannot be ignored; which, unavoidably, must be *dealt with*.

" I do not know you, sir. I really cannot stand here conversing with a perfect stranger." Then, with a little, half-doubting glance up to the fine eyes: " Are you one of the O'Hagans of Dunnamore ? "

O'Hagan bowed as no other man, though you search the courts of Europe, can bow.

" Then, Captain O'Hagan, since you are a gentleman, please forget about the doorporter. Believe me, I have troubles enough without seeking new ones."

There was pathos in the words, in her low, quivering voice.

" I cannot doubt it. And, since you know my family, you may know that its name stands stainless for seven generations. You should not be here, at this hour, alone. In the absence of a father, of a brother, accept my escort. It is in no way encumbent upon you to accept my friendship, though it would be devoted and disinterested."

She was biting her lip now, in pathetic perplexity; but there was a new confidence in the glance which she gave him. It was the glance of a woman who sorely lacked a friend, and into whose heart the conviction was stealing that heaven had sent her one.

"You are more than kind, Captain O'Hagan." Now she met his eyes frankly. Her decision was made. "I am—Lady Brian Dillon."

("You see, Raymond," he has since explained to me, "there was more than mere chance in my unaccountable decision to explore that passage. Fate, my boy—fate!")

He took the gloved hand which she offered with a pretty embarrassment, and bent over it in his unique, courtier fashion.

"I have never met your husband, Lady Dillon. But his late father, Sir John, was one of my dearest friends. I regard you, now, as that dear friend's daughter, and since

Fate has brought us both here to-night, I regard your interests as a sacred charge. You are in trouble. How can I serve you?"

II.

AT THE STAGE DOOR.

I DOUBT if London could furnish another man—a father confessor excepted—who, in so brief a time, could have learnt from the young Lady Dillon so much of her history as did O'Hagan. Side by side, they paced up and down a comparatively quiet street dipping riverward, and the girl (for she was no more) confided in this man, whom, twenty minutes earlier, she had not known.

Does not that argue eloquently for my friend? Does it not make amends for much that seems harsh in his nature? For although, alas! women often are deceived in men, a woman's instincts can never err in such case as this; a true woman, as this one, never pours out the trouble with which her heart is bursting, to a knave—to a blackguard. I defy you to confute me. Be it remembered that, by a trick of Fate—or shall we say Providence?—these two had friends in common. Nor be it forgot that, for fifty miles north, south, east and west of Dunnamore, " the honour of an O'Hagan " is a form of oath. But, nevertheless, I maintain that there is something grandly and expansively human—something splendid and true—in the nature of a man whom at such brief acquaintance a good woman *knows* to be worthy of her confidence. Don't you agree with me?

"Of course I remember your wedding!" said O'Hagan. "Bless my soul! you were a Miss Sheila Cavanagh! As a child you must have been at Dunnamore many a time! Why! we are quite old friends! You are not married three months, yet?"

"Ten weeks," replied Lady Dillon, pathetically.

HE BURIES AN OLD LOVE 133

" And simply because your husband, Sir Brian, saw you walking in St. James's Park with a gentleman——"

" He has not spoken to me—for four days ! "—brokenly.

" And now he is waiting on the stage of the Novelty for a Miss Betty Chatterton, late of the Folly Theatre, whom formerly he admired——"

"—He used to go about with her a lot, I know ! "

" And this gentleman with whom you were walking ? "

Lady Dillon looked away.

" Ah," said O'Hagan sadly, " you have been indiscreet. He was an old admirer ? " (nod). " Persistent, unscrupulous ? " (nod)— " and you were sending this fellow about his business ? "

She looked up to him as, of old, looked Menippus Lycius to Apollonius of Tyana ; as to one omniscient—yet, crowning wonder, as to a favourite brother. Such is the timbre of my friend's exquisite sympathy. Is it not a divine gift ?

"How can you possibly know that?"

"My dear Lady Dillon—you have told me! Does your husband know this person?"

"He knows *of* him. But he has never even asked me his name. I thought he understood that I did not care and never had cared for the man. Oh! why did I see him? Why did I see him? But I feared that, unless I definitely dismissed him, he would compromise me!"

"My poor child!" He patted her arm, soothingly. There are phases of his patronage which are healing. One absorbs his condescension gratefully, as a penitent receiving absolution from a holy cardinal. "You see, your marriage was a family arrangement, and your husband is uncertain of your affections. This regrettable incident has convinced him—wrongly—that from your point of view it is merely a *mariage de convenance*. His flirtation is a harmless one. He is, I dare swear, eating his heart out! But the pride of the Dillons has him by the throat. My dear little lady—leave him to me!"

HE BURIES AN OLD LOVE 135

She looked up to him wonderingly again; but, with something of the touching confidence of a child, permitted him to conduct her Strandward.

"Captain O'Hagan! I could never, never explain to him! That is why I dare not speak! He would *never* forgive me for seeing him again—would never understand——"

"Leave it entirely in my hands! *I* will do the explaining! Simply accept my explanation, and decline in any way to enlarge upon it. You shall not be compromised, because I know you do not deserve it. Neither shall that hare-brained husband of yours compromise another girl out of mere *pique*."

She said nothing to that. In the Strand, opposite the Novelty:

"That is your car yonder?" asked O'Hagan.

"Oh! don't let Priestman see me!" cried Lady Dillon. "I was afraid he would see me when I spoke to that wretch at the door!"

"You are perfectly certain that your husband is in the theatre?"

"Yes! yes! I don't know why I asked that man! But, indeed, I don't know what possessed me at all! Oh! Captain O'Hagan, I am so miserable!"

"Boy!" said O'Hagan to a passing urchin—"tell the chauffeur of the Rolls Royce yonder, to pull around here!"

Off ran the boy.

"But——" began Lady Dillon.

O'Hagan patted her arm. The chauffeur, having received the boy's message, could be seen looking in their direction. Presently he walked across to where they stood. Recognising Lady Dillon, he stared; then touched his cap.

"I ordered you to bring the car over," said O'Hagan, icily.

"Sir Brian"—— began the man.

"Did you understand my words?"

The chauffeur ran back, and in a few moments the big car was drawn up to the kerb. O'Hagan placed Lady Dillon comfortably in a cushioned corner.

HE BURIES AN OLD LOVE 137

"Good-night, dear Lady Dillon," he said. "I will bring Brian home to you very shortly!"

Her wondering, tearful eyes never left his face. To the now deferential though badly embarrassed man:

"Home!" said O'Hagan.

Off moved the smoothly-running car. Whilst she could see him where he stood, Lady Dillon never took her eyes from the tall, cloaked figure of this old friend of old friends and one so newly found, of this astonishing Samaritan who had promised to restore to her the gladness of life. With picturesque head bowed he waited until the Rolls Royce was lost from view, one gloved hand resting upon the heavy ebony cane, the other, ungloved, dangling from two long fingers the monocle dependent on its black silk ribbon.

It is a never-ending source of regret to me that we have no Velasquez to-day. Captain the Hon. Bernard O'Hagan would inspire such an one to a great masterpiece.

My friend returned to the narrow alley-way,

descended it, and stood before the unofficial deputy for the baggage-man, whose treatment of Lady Dillon had occasioned his just resentment. In his dealings with such as this, O'Hagan can be terrible. To him he addressed no word.

Dropping his monocle, he seized the fellow by the ear (with his gloved hand) and dragged the agonised face closely to his own haughty countenance. The feat was seemingly performed effortless—such is the outstanding wonder of that Judo, or Higher Jiu-Jitsu, whereof Shashu Myuku of Nagasaki is the Grand Master. There are not six Europeans, O'Hagan will tell you, who have been initiated into the occultry of the Japanese super-force.

"You recently insulted a lady who inquired if Sir Brian Dillon had entered the stage-door. Down on your knees, you sot—and beg for pardon!"

Obedient to a power which, seemingly entering at the ear, proceeded thence through every tortured nerve of his person, rendering him helpless, inert, down dropped the big, hulking figure. It chanced that none was

HE BURIES AN OLD LOVE 139

there to see. Yet the exhibition was an odd one.

"Repeat, after me, 'I humbly beg, sir——'"

"Police!" gasped the man, and strove to get at O'Hagan with his hands.

Abruptly he dropped them; his big face grew livid. The Captain, holding the ear in that vice-grip, had merely turned it slightly backward. The man groaned; beads of perspiration started on his brow.

"Repeat, after me, 'I humbly beg, sir, for the lady's pardon.'"

Faintly:

"I humbly . . . beg, sir . . . for . . . my Gawd! . . . the lidy's pardon!"

"And abjectly entreat you to forgive me!"

"And . . . abjec . . . abjec'y entreat . . . you to forgive . . . me!"

"Get up!"

The victim struggled erect. He met the quelling gaze.

"Any repetition of the offence means that my man will wait upon you—and bring a horse-whip!"

The fellow scrambled aside, and raised a quivering hand to his forehead. Captain O'Hagan, swinging his monocle, strode to the stage-door.

III.

IN THE DRESSING-ROOM.

To the stage-door keeper said O'Hagan:
"Has Miss Chatterton appeared yet?"
"She has, sir."
"Is she in her dressing-room?"
"I believe so, sir."
"Has she a private dressing-room?"
"Yes, sir."
"Is she dressed, yet?"
"She must be, sir. She finished over half-an-hour ago, and a gentleman went up some time since."
"What number is her room?"

HE BURIES AN OLD LOVE

"It's Number Six, sir, but——"

Captain O'Hagan placed half-a-crown upon the window-ledge and stepped along the passage.

"Excuse me, sir!" The man came running from his box.

O'Hagan turned, glass raised.

"You wished to speak to me?"

"Thank you very much, sir, but I must take your card through first, or——"

"My name is Captain O'Hagan. I have business with Miss Chatterton."

He proceeded, unruffled.

"You'll get me into trouble, sir——"

O'Hagan, over his shoulder:

"I esteem your regard for duty, my man. Rely upon me."

He was gone. The door-keeper scratched his head.

Ascending a flight of stone steps, the Captain came to a landing, a door opening upon it. The door was ajar and bore no number, but voices might be heard proceeding from the room beyond. O'Hagan rapped, and opened the door.

Several gentlemen, in several stages of undress, all looked up from their several toilettes.

"I fear I intrude," said O'Hagan, holding his monocle before his right eye and examining the occupants of the apartment with a kind of genial curiosity. "I wish to find room number six."

"Next floor, second door," volunteered a young man in underwear.

"I am indebted."

O'Hagan withdrew and proceeded upstairs. Room six showed a closed door. O'Hagan knocked.

"Who's there?" inquired a masculine voice.

O'Hagan entered.

A golden-headed lady, who was arranging a rare exotic in hats upon her elaborate coiffure, fixed wondering eyes upon the intruder. A maid glanced up from where she knelt beside a large basket; and a dark-haired, perfectly groomed young man, of military bearing, rose hurriedly from his seat upon a second and even larger basket.

HE BURIES AN OLD LOVE

Captain O'Hagan bowed

"Miss Chatterton, your pardon. Sir Brian Dillon, I presume? Might I ask you, my good girl"—to the staring maid—"to withdraw."

He held the door open.

"Here, I say!" burst out Miss Chatterton. "Who are you? What's it all about——"

"I am Captain O'Hagan. I have a family matter to discuss with Sir Brian; and I wish you, Miss Chatterton, to be present."

He waved his monocle towards the maid, and then in the direction of the open door. The girl stood up, looked at her mistress, but saw her to be as helpless as herself; looked at the forceful new arrival, and slowly went out. O'Hagan closed the door. Two pairs of wondering eyes followed his every movement. My friend has a singular quality of personality. I believe he could so enter the House of Lords as to visit consternation upon every peer present, and to set the bishops reviewing their pasts with grave misgivings. Bernard O'Hagan is a mannerist of genius.

Sir Brian Dillon cleared his throat.

"If I might venture on a remark," he said, with an angry gleam in his grey eyes, "what do you want, and who the devil *are* you?"

O'Hagan wound the black ribbon about his right forefinger.

"I am the gentleman," he replied, with frigid distinctness, "whom you saw walking with Lady Dillon in St. James's Park some days ago, and I am here to *demand* an explanation!"

Have you sometimes, at a proper and sombre social function, dreamed of what would happen if some bold spirit rose up and sang one of Mr. George Robey's sprightliest songs? Have you even contemplated, in what I may term horrified delight, the effect of a loudly uttered swear-word upon a gathering of elders? This remark of O'Hagan's produced that sort of effect.

Betty Chatterton slowly sank down into an armchair, never removing her gaze from the last speaker. Sir Brian's eyes opened wider and yet wider. He bit his lower lip—and took a step forward. He halted.

"*You*," he began—and his tone was different

HE BURIES AN OLD LOVE 145

from that of his normal speech—" *you* are here, to demand an explanation of *me* ! You admit that you are——"

" I beg," O'Hagan interrupted him, " that you will not refer to my statement as an admission. I am proud of my name, and proud of my friendship with your wife. You have wronged her, and you wrong Miss Chatterton. Particularly, you have wronged *me*. It is for this—for your gross insult to myself—that I am here to call you to account ! "

Dillon nearly choked ; and his fingers twitched convulsively. He believed, and with a large and generous trust had sought no word from his wife in aye or nay, that it had been another than himself who first had won her love. Later, he believed that his trust had been misplaced, had been betrayed ; that the unknown who had played some part, great or small, in her life before he, Brian, came into it, was indeed lord of the kingdom that he madly had thought his own.

Now the usurper stood before him, his attitude neither apologetic nor explanatory—

not that of the offender but of the offended!
"—To call me to account!" echoed Dillon, in a voice sunken almost to a whisper.

That form of words was the crowning affront of all. It summoned into being the primeval savage which dwells somewhere within every man of Celtic stock. It was this primitive being, whose tribal pride had stifled relenting—denied the woman fair speech and trial—and not the cultured modern man, with whom O'Hagan was come to deal.

"Betty"—Dillon's speech was thick as that of a drunkard—"would you mind postponing the supper?" He swallowed, dryly. "I will see you—to the car. Forgive me, but to-night——"

"*I* will see Miss Chatterton to a cab," interrupted O'Hagan's icy voice. "I have sent Lady Dillon home in the car. *You* will await me here——"

Dillon clenched his fists: his nostrils dilated. In that instant my friend came more nearly to an unseemly embroilment than ever in his surprising career.

HE BURIES AN OLD LOVE

"Brian!"

Betty Chatterton sprang to Dillon, clutching his arm.

"Miss Chatterton," continued O'Hagan, "I beg you to accept my escort. It will be better if we go at once."

She looked from man to man, and grew pale to the lips. Sir Brian glassily stared directly at O'Hagan and ignored the hand that clung to his rigid arm. The girl released her clasp and turned imploring blue eyes upon the Captain.

"Oh, Captain O'Hagan," she said, "there is some dreadful mistake! If you think— ah! how can I say what I mean? *Will* you believe me "—she frankly met his gaze— "if I tell you that Sir Brian and I are just chums?" Her eyes were flooded with tears. "He is awfully—dreadfully unhappy about . . ." She laid her hand hesitatingly upon O'Hagan's arm. "I know you have done him no wrong. Won't you believe *me*, too? Can't we be friends?"

("I had anticipated something altogether more vulgar, Raymond," O'Hagan recently informed me. " I will confess that I was surprised and delighted. Miss Chatterton had the instincts of a lady and the generosity of a gentleman! A really lovable nature, my boy. That infernal ass deserved nothing so fine as her friendship!")

The Captain raised her hand to his lips, bending over it with stately courtesy. Again their eyes met—and these two understood one another.

"Betty," began Dillon, advancing.

She turned to him.

"Stay where you are, Brian," she said, with a sudden note of command. "You must see that I don't want to be mixed up in your quarrels. And—Captain O'Hagan is right. We cannot expect the world to understand us. You shouldn't have come here to-night. No, I'm not angry with you, silly boy—but it wasn't fair to me. I can see that, now. You had nearly made a big mistake, Brian. Good-bye."

She held out her hand, firmly. Dillon turned away.

"All right," she said, and shrugged her

shoulders. "You'll know I was a real pal one day."

She leant lightly upon O'Hagan's arm; and the two left the room. She smiled bravely as they passed the stage door-keeper and bade him cheerily good-night.

("Gad, Raymond!" says O'Hagan, "that girl was a brick; for she was every bit as much in love with Dillon as Dillon was in love with his wife!")

IV.

THE SNOWS OF THE YUKON.

O'HAGAN, with some research, recently established the fact, in the case of Betty Chatterton, that "there was good blood on the mother's side." I fancy he slept better after that. As a child of the people (I use my friend's phraseology) Miss Chatterton was a disturbing element in the Captain's philosophy.

He turned to the dressing-room. Let us accompany him.

On the landing stood the maid.

"Please, sir," said she, timidly, "may I go in and finish packing the basket?"

"Presently, my good girl," replied the Captain, "presently."

Sir Brian Dillon was seated where O'Hagan first had found him. He was smoking a cigarette. His face was somewhat pale.

He rose, as the Captain entered, and very deliberately threw the cigarette into the tiny hearth. To any but a student of indications, he must have appeared quite composed. O'Hagan knew it to be otherwise. Yet he was unprepared for Dillon's action. Dillon, silently, leapt at him across the room!

I say he was unprepared. In a certain sense he was. But, on the other hand, a pupil of Myuku is never unprepared. O'Hagan dropped his cane, instinctively (the Higher Jiu-Jitsu is essentially instinctive). He grasped the fist which whizzed within half an inch of his right ear, performing one of those lightning movements unachievable

HE BURIES AN OLD LOVE 151

by any other man of my acquaintance. He thrust it up. He twisted it to the right—down—and doubled the arm behind Dillon's back. Daintily, he clasped the other wrist and held the left arm inert, outstretched at an angle of forty-five from his opponent's side.

This, you may know, is a simple trick, which can be performed, with luck, by several members, *individually, of the Metropolitan and City Police forces.

Dillon made one attempt to break away—and then stood still, looking back across his shoulder at O'Hagan.

" By God, I'll kill you ! "

There was something shocking in the murderous intent which beaconed from his eyes.

" Later, you shall be afforded every opportunity. But, first, you must hear me. Shall I release you ? "

No humiliation can equal that which it is in the power of the expert Jiu-Jitsuist to nflict. An enraged man, though he be outclassed, overweighted, may fight to the last and keep his pride. But this supreme inertia, this being petrified, posed as for a ballroom scene in a "living-picture," with frenzied anger boiling in the veins and no muscle responding to the mind's urgent commands, is something that must be experienced fully to be appreciated.

Dillon panted.

"If I release you," added O'Hagan icily, "it will be upon parole; upon the understanding that you conserve your resentment for a more fitting time."

"Release me!"

"Upon that understanding?"

"Curse you! . . . *yes*!"

O'Hagan dropped his hands, stepped back to the little mantelpiece and leaned upon it, raising his monocle before his right eye.

"Sir Brian Dillon," he said deliberately, "you may have heard my name; for I knew your father well."

The other's fingers twitched. He glared directly at O'Hagan, and thrust his hands deeply in his pockets.

"Your father would have known the gross

HE BURIES AN OLD LOVE 153

nature of your insult to me. Strong man as you are, he would have forced you to apologise, or have knocked you down. Do your memories bear me out?"

Dillon swallowed, emotionally.

"You add insult to the most awful injury one man can inflict upon another——"

"Stop!" O'Hagan's big eyes blazed. He took a step forward. "Stop! By God, sir, if you presume to cast such an innuendo in my face I will break your neck, though I hang for it!"

There was a species of subdued ferocity in his manner that had forced conviction upon anyone. No man born of woman could have doubted him.

"You slander me. It is no excuse that you do so, thinking I am he who died on the Yukon border last March."

A puzzled expression mingled and conflicted with the others which flitted across Dillon's face.

"Since Sheila Cavanagh and I met at Dunnamore Castle—a childish meeting which your wife had forgotten—we never had set eyes upon each other until that day in St. James's Park. Despite the passage of years, I knew her again. How dare you—I repeat, sir, how dare you presume to deny me the privilege of your wife's friendship!"

Dillon's expression changed again—to one of bewilderment.

"Then," he gasped, "you are not——"

O'Hagan raised his head.

"Let him rest in peace," he said sternly. "He was an honourable man, unfortunate in love. You wrong him villainously. If she had cared for him he would be alive to-day. It was something very like suicide—and therefore I charge you, Brian Dillon, never to breathe a word of his unhappy end, never to speak his name to your wife."

"I don't know his name. How do you——"

"I buried him in the snow!" said Captain O'Hagan with impressive finality.

Dillon dropped limply on to the big property-basket.

"Then Sheila never cared for him! And he is dead! And it was you, an old friend, and a friend of my father's, whom——"

HE BURIES AN OLD LOVE

"You have been a villain to her!—a villain to Miss Chatterton—doubly a villain to me!——"

Sir Brian sprang up, his face boyish, bright with a glad contrition.

"Captain O'Hagan!" he cried, "will you take my hand? A hundred thousand times I apologise! *Can* you forgive me! Do you think Sheila can?"

* * * * *

"At such times," my mendacious friend has informed me, "to lie becomes a virtue. Dillon distrusted his wife's old admirer—whose name he had quixotically, though fortunately, avoided learning. Therefore, preparatory to peace, the anonymous gentleman had to be whitewashed. His whitewashing accomplished, next, in order to insure Dillon's silence respecting his history, he had to be buried for ever.

"I buried him in the eternal snows, Raymond. What more appropriate tomb for the rejected lover?"

EXPLOIT THE FIFTH.

HE DEALS WITH DON JUAN.

EXPLOIT THE FIFTH.

HE DEALS WITH DON JUAN.

I.

HAVERLEY OF THE GREYS.

My friend Captain O'Hagan is a man fatally easy to misjudge; a man monstrously difficult to appreciate. Arraign him before a bar of his peers, and no two findings would march in step, no two voices be in unison. If we except the critic of the *Tailor and Cutter*, I doubt, indeed, if there be a man in London who perceives the exquisite distinction of O'Hagan's dress. His mode of going hatless is dubbed affectation; his purple-lined cloak an ostentatious extravagance.

But some there are who instinctively detect O'Hagan's sterling qualities; some (as myself) achieve to this knowledge; and some have it thrust upon them.

I recall an illustrative incident:

O'Hagan and I were at one of those pleasant afternoon functions where the caller surreptitiously, but constantly, glances at his timepiece in order to learn if a sufficient interval has elapsed since his arrival to admit of his departure. You have been, no doubt? O'Hagan rarely goes; but a Miss Pamela Crichton was present on this occasion—and, somehow, O'Hagan and I are frequently meeting this charming girl at all sorts of odd places—quite by accident, oh, quite by accident.

"I am proud of the success which Pamela has achieved," my friend whispered to me, "since I took her up." (She composes). "But I do not approve of her accepting these social invitations. She is merely providing the hostess with a gratuitous entertainment."

This view of the matter, from O'Hagan, surprised me. But later, the hostess said:

"*Dear* Miss Crichton, you will play us that last charming piece of yours, *won't* you!"

Mrs. Pointzby-North's request was sweetly proffered, but it was a sweetness akin to that with which, addressing a valued butler, she might have said:

"*Milton*, you will see that the bull-dogs are not permitted to fight in the drawing-room in future, *won't* you!"

O'Hagan did not object to the tone of patronage, however. ("Mrs. Pointzby-North," said he, "is a member of a very old and distinguished family." That, of course, was final.)

But when Pamela began to play, delightfully, and everyone continued to chatter, simianly, he stood up.

"Rank has its obligations," he said—and strode across to the player.

He took both her hands, and the flow of melody ceased upon an unexpected discord. Then came silence—the thrilling silence of surprise. Lolling gracefully upon the baby grand, my friend toyed with the black ribbon upon which his monocle dangles and glanced toward Mrs. Pointzby-North.

"My dear Mrs. North, as a very old and

quite absurdly privileged friend, might I address a few words to everybody, without annoyance to you?"

Mrs. Pointzby-North, fluttering somewhat:

"My *dear* Captain O'Hagan! As if you *could* offend me, however hard you tried!"

O'Hagan inclined his head, and raised the monocle to survey the expectant ring of guests. Then:

"Good folks, Miss Pamela Crichton is so well worth listening to, that I beg you will preserve a perfect quiet whilst she is playing. Believe me, you will be well repaid, and will furthermore confer upon Mrs. North and upon myself a favour which we shall deeply appreciate!"

Pamela performed amid a throbbing silence which would have gratified Sarah Bernhardt. But I divined how in future the doors of Mrs. Pointzby-North would be closed to Miss Crichton.

("It is better," O'Hagan explained to me, when we had seen the girl to a cab. "I do not desire that Pamela be treated as a public exhibit.")

Replace the famous cloak with a toga, and in O'Hagan you have a very complete patrician—an aristocrat of sensibilities so exquisite that the trifling errors of good society jar upon them more harshly than the eating of peas with a knife upon the atrophied perceptions of the merely respectable.

After dinner that evening Sir Roger Rundel called upon O'Hagan in his chambers.

My friend's chambers overlook Whitehall, and, in his moments of ease, he is always to be found in the room which he calls his library, but whose appointments more nearly correspond with those of a harêm. To visitors but superficially acquainted with O'Hagan, this apartment proves a surprise. Its arabesques dimly perceptible in the blue rays of a hanging lamp, the plash of water in a tiny marble basin enhancing the illusion that one has lost one's way, this *mandarah* possesses all the charms of the unexpected.

For golden carp in the basin you are of course prepared? Prepare, further, for O'Hagan in a loose blue robe, O'Hagan extended upon a cushioned divan, sipping coffee from a tiny porcelain cup and enjoying the solace of tumbâk in a Persian narghli.

Donohue, a model man, immaculate, in immaculate black, proclaimed the arrival, and ushered in the person, of Sir Roger. You would like Sir Roger Rundel; bronzed, well groomed, reserved, forty-five; he is what we mean by a typical English gentleman.

He and O'Hagan are old friends. Donohue made fresh *kahweh* (no one expects whisky in the *mandarah*), whilst Sir Roger selected from the rack an amber mouthpiece neatly labelled "R.R." and appropriated the guest's tube of the narghli.

O'Hagan: "Been hoping to see you every day since I heard of your return, Rundel."

Sir Roger: "Yes, yes. Since my—marriage, **fear** I've neglected bachelor friends. I leave London to-night—on departmental business."

Silence; broken by bubbling of narghli. Enter Donohue with coffee. Exit Donohue.

O'Hagan fumbled for the indispensable pebble, found it, and examined Sir Roger's face critically.

HE DEALS WITH DON JUAN 165

"There's a fly in the ointment, Rundel. Name the brute's species."

Sir Roger put down his cup with a rattle.

"Captain Haverley," he snapped—"and now I've said it!"

"Ah," mused O'Hagan; "Haverley, of the —th Greys. Only know him by repute."

"What sort of repute?" growled Rundel.

"Yes," O'Hagan nodded, and dropped his monocle. "*That* sort!"

Sir Roger got upon his feet, and began to pace up and down a square of Persian carpet.

"We know one another, O'Hagan. There's not another man in England I'd confide in. But—well—Beesley told me about this afternoon—at Mrs. Pointzby-North's, and I said, 'Same old O'Hagan!' That's what it is, O'Hagan: there's only one of you—only one of you! This—friendship—between my wife and Haverley is nothing—from Val's point of view. Understand? *She* means no harm."

"What attitude have you adopted?"

"No attitude. Overlooked it. But I'm going away; and I will *not* have Val talked about, and I will *not* be made to look ridiculous. In a word, O'Hagan, I'll have no damned *cavalière servante* with Haverley's reputation dangling after my wife!"

"Well?" said O'Hagan, calmly sipping coffee.

"Val's younger than me; and I don't want her to think that *I* think—see what I mean? I can't speak to *her*."

"I follow you perfectly," said O'Hagan. "You can speak to neither party without the risk of precipitating what you wish to avoid. Thanks for entrusting this matter to me, Rundel. I will call out Captain Haverley to-morrow morning!"

"My dear fellow! never do at all!"

"Why? I should see to it that he remained incapacitated in France throughout the term of your absence!"

"Too medieval, O'Hagan—too dam' medieval. Bar you the country for twelve months at least! Besides, he might refuse —or, worse, you might kill him!"

"True," agreed O'Hagan; "such mistakes have occurred. However—if Captain

Haverley is not permitted the society of Lady Rundel during your absence, I take it that you will be satisfied?"

"Certainly! certainly! If I knew that——"

"Rely upon it, Rundel," said O'Hagan, rising. "I will put an end to this undesirable intimacy. I shall regard it as my sacred duty to do so!"

In that moment he was superb; a man worthy of the confidence of kings; a man to hold stainless the honour of a queen.

"My dear fellow!" said Sir Roger, and shook his hand furiously. "My dear, dear fellow!"

Ah! what a privilege it is to call Bernard O'Hagan your friend!

II.

ACCORDING TO MYUKU.

Captain Haverley placed upon a table beside him the card of Captain The Hon. Bernard O'Hagan, V.C., D.S.O., as that distinguished officer was shown in.

"Of course I have heard of you, Captain O'Hagan," he said; "but this is our first meeting, I think?" He glanced at his watch. "Better late than never!"

O'Hagan bowed coldly.

"I was about to refer to my calling upon you at this late hour," he explained; "but since you have so rudely anticipated me, an apology becomes unnecessary. I will merely state my business."

Haverley, a blonde and arrogantly handsome man at whose breast Eros aimed his darts every time that he went into a drawing-room, and at whose back fifty per cent. of his company were sworn to aim their rifles the first time that he went into action, believed that he had misunderstood O'Hagan. But:

"In short," continued the latter, swinging his monocle, "your friendship with Lady Rundel must cease. It will be evident to you that in her husband's absence its continuance would be compromising."

Haverley knew, then, that he had heard aright, and his face paled with an anger which was intense; his hazel eyes seemed to emit sparks; and he slowly moved nearer to this adept in polished insult.

"Captain O'Hagan," he said, distinctly—"the door is immediately behind you."

"A matter of more pressing import," replied O'Hagan icily, "is immediately in front of me."

With three swinging strides he crossed to the mantelpiece. It was decorated with several women's photographs—among them, one of Lady Rundel. Snatching it, framed as it was, from its place, he broke it across his knee and hurled the fragments into the hearth!

At that, Haverley leapt. Calculating with a boxer's cunning the exact instant when his man would turn, he launched a blow for the angle of his jaw. The primitive, strong within him, ruled now supreme. But O'Hagan did *not* turn.

He stepped back upon Haverley, and stooped.

It is needless to quote the apposite precept of Shashu Myuku of Nagasaki (Dean of the College of Higher Jiu-Jitsu) in order to make clear what happened. Haverley performed a complete somersault over O'Hagan's arched back and fell, heaped up, crashing in the hearth.

Captain O'Hagan stepped to the door, and gained it as Haverley's man hurriedly entered.

"You understand?" said O'Hagan. "I forbid you this lady's company. If you dispute my right to do so, I shall expect your friends in the morning."

Haverley, choking, shaken, got upon his feet. His white-faced man barred the door.

"Excuse me, sir . . ."

O'Hagan brushed him aside. He has a sweeping motion of the left arm which would remove a lifeguardsman from his path as

HE DEALS WITH DON JUAN 171

effectively as the flick of a handkerchief brushes a fly from a bald head.

The man clutched at a buhl cabinet to save himself. Upon a discordant finale of smashing porcelain, intermingled with human cursing, Captain O'Hagan made his exit to the plaudit of the gods.

He is a master of effective curtains.

III.

INTRODUCING DONOHUE.

I HAVE hinted, I think, that my friend disapproves of many usages of modern society. He maintains that it is in no sense representative of the true aristocracy. (" I have known a knight, Raymond," he says, " who avoided eating water-melon because it made his ears wet.") This anecdote I take to be more properly a parable; but it serves to illustrate a phase of O'Hagan's character.

He would have the feminine section of society composed wholly of Cæsars' wives. How he reconciles this view with the career of the fair O'Hagan who embellished a Stuart Court held at Hampton, I am too diffident to inquire though curious to know.

His espousal of the righteous cause of Sir Roger Rundel was in every sense a love-match. What advice should *you* have offered to Sir Roger? At best your aid had ceased with words, I dare to predict. But from the first traceable O'Hagan (some kind of pirate, I believe) to Bernard, the O'Hagans essentially figure as men of action, often as not of sanguinary action. We are agreed, then, that you and I are not of the kidney properly to conduct this affair? Your attention for Captain Bernard O'Hagan!

No communication from Haverley reached him during the following morning. ("I have since taken occasion to look up the fellow's pedigree," O'Hagan informed me; "and the fortunes of the family apparently date from

HE DEALS WITH DON JUAN

a certain pork butcher by letters patent to George III. One can understand a lack of finesse in a scion of sausage-mongers. God help the Army!")

Noon, and after, saw my friend engaged upon affairs of his own. But in the evening Donohue reported in the *mandarah*.

This remarkable man is worthy of a brief inspection.

In figure he is sturdy, of no more than medium height. He has well-brushed hair of the colour of stale mustard, and a ruddy complexion. Clean-shaven, his upper lip usurps an undue share of his countenance, and his jaw would spell truculence were its significance not modified by the humorous twinkle in the sky-blue eyes.

Behold Donohue, a man of attainments; a valet unsurpassable, of eye more true for the fold of a cloak than any modiste of the Rue de la Paix; a colourist in whom discord between a scarf and a soft shirt produces a blanching of the cheek; who, of a hundred waistcoats, having a hundred shades, will nnerringly select *the* waistcoat for *the* occasion. He has other qualities, to be displayed later.

Donohue : " Sir."

" Well, Donohue ? "—O'Hagan.

" Captain Haverley, with Lady Rundel, at Folly Theatre ; stalls ; Row B ; numbers 6 and 7."

" Very good."

Exit Donohue.

This paragon must have delighted the gloomy soul of Athos.

Bernard O'Hagan, having finished his coffee, discarded the loose robe for the purple-lined cloak, pulled on his gloves, and sallied forth into Whitehall, cloak flying, holding his cane like an Italian rapier, and generally comporting himself as some Buckingham bound for St. James's.

He turned his steps in the direction of the Folly, however. To the box-office clerk :

" I require a stall."

" We have only three vacant, sir."

" One will be sufficient."

No traffic of the stage that evening had

HE DEALS WITH DON JUAN 175

created anything approximating to the impression occasioned by O'Hagan's entrance. My friend has been called a *poseur*. It is unjust. He cannot help it. Bernard O'Hagan belongs to the age of plumes and velvet. His is the soul of a true courtier.

Just within the big glass door he paused for a moment, and, the monocle glittering as he held it before his right eye, studied the occupants of Row B. Perceiving Lady Rundel (a conspicuously pretty woman) staring at him fascinatedly, he bowed. A hundred sighs arose; a hundred hearts lay unheeded at the feet of this incomparable cavalier.

Haverley devoted his attention exclusively to the stage. He was gnawing his moustache.

Throughout the performance, O'Hagan lolled back in his stall, one leg negligently thrown across the other, and studied the ladies, who constitute the principal attraction of this house, with a kind of bored curiosity.

At the close of the play Lady Rundel and

Captain Haverley stood in the lobby. O'Hagan bowed low before madame. Then, to her squire:

"I believe I forbade you this lady's society, sir?" said he.

There are simple remarks which, at certain times, you or I might make, but which you and I lack the stark audacity to make. Made, they strike the listener with a species of paralysis. This was one of them.

Lady Rundel flushed, and started back.

"Captain O'Hagan!" she began——

"Don't speak to him, Lady Rundel!" came hissing, forced speech from Haverley. "Allow me to see you to your car. I have something very particular to say to Captain O'Hagan!"

O'Hagan bowed again inimitably.

"Good-night, Lady Rundel. I have something very particular to say to *you* in the morning."

Captain O'Hagan sank reposefully into a lounge, and, the observed of everyone who passed out of the theatre, awaited Haverley's return. At least a score of ladies inquired *sotto voce* of their escorts: " Who is that distinguished-looking man ? "

Haverley presently returned, forcing his way roughly against the thinning stream of supper-seekers. Over the heads of the outgoing, O'Hagan perceived the drawn face and angry, blazing eyes. He turned his glass casually in that direction.

Quivering before him, Haverley said, with hardly repressed violence :

" You are a blackguard ! I have little doubt that a public brawl would be to your low taste. But I prefer to call upon you to-morrow. I shall bring a horse-whip ! "

Unable further to trust himself to face the icy stare which met him, he turned, and almost ran from the now empty lobby.

Captain O'Hagan swung streetward, in turn. A taxi-cab had at that moment pulled up to the kerb ; and Haverley was fumbling with shaking fingers for a coin for the theatre attendant, ere entering it.

O'Hagan calmly opened the door, stepped in, and reclosed it. Leaning from the window :

"Junior Guards Club!" he said. "Half a sovereign if you do it in four minutes!"

Gold is a talisman, my masters. The taxi-driver risked consequences—and started.

("You see," goes O'Hagan's explanation of this episode, "the cab was the last in the rank, and I had an appointment. Haverley may have had one also. But pedigree before pork, Raymond.")

IV.

DONOHUE'S ORDERS.

THE morning was young, and O'Hagan discussing rolls and coffee when Donohue announced Captain Haverley and Mr. Salter.

O'Hagan rose ceremoniously. He wore a slate-grey lounge suit, with a silver-grey plush French knot in lieu of a tie. This combination suits him admirably and affords Donohue great scope for discrimination in the selecting of a soft shirt to harmonise with the scheme.

Entered Haverley, accompanied by a tall and preternaturally thin gentleman who carried a leather case. O'Hagan bowed coldly to the captain, and upon his companion turned the monocle.

"This," he said frigidly, sweeping his hand toward Mr. Salter, "I assume to be your horsewhip?"

"Mr Salter is my solicitor!" replied Haverley loudly. "I have decided that a public exposure is what you require! We have therefore——"

(O'Hagan pressed a bell.)

"——I say we have therefore called formally to advise you——"

(Donohue entered.)

"——That a police-court summons for drunken assault and——"

O'Hagan, waving monocle Salterward:

"Donohue, kindly see this person to the door."

Mr. Salter, who was opening his brief-case looked up alarmedly.

"My solicitor," shouted Haverley, who was rapidly losing control of himself, "is——"

"Donohue!"

Donohue bowed to Mr. Salter and held wide the door.

Salter: "Captain O'Hagan, as legal adviser——"

"*Donohue!*"

Donohue stepped forward and took up Mr. Salter's case. Within his right arm he linked the left of Mr. Salter, and with the gentle firmness of a Milo of Crotona led him rapidly from the room. Came a quavering cry:

"You will pay dearly for this insult!"

Haverley, eyes aflame, bounded to the door. It was locked. He turned to where O'Hagan, lolling against the mantelpiece, studied the morning's manœuvres through upraised glass.

"I do not," explained O'Hagan icily, "allow solicitors in these chambers."

Haverley leant back against the door, almost as though he were preparing for a

HE DEALS WITH DON JUAN 181

spring. He was a man swept by a tornado of passion, and before its force he quivered and shook.

"The law is the weapon of churls," continued O'Hagan. "You are a soldier—as I regret to remind you. Upon the table on your right are French foils, Italian rapiers, and three types of sabre. You clearly maintain your right to Lady Rundel's society. I forbid you to see her again. We will settle the point."

Haverley cleared his throat, and spoke huskily:

"You are a madman—and I will see that you are treated as such——"

"Before we commence," added O'Hagan, taking up a writing-block, "we will each write a note to the effect that we were practising a new mode of mounted attack, and that the affair was an accident. One of these notes will afterwards be destroyed."

"Open the door!" demanded Haverley, tensely.

Captain O'Hagan observed him with a kind of unpleasant curiosity.

"As a soldier, and as a gentleman, you cannot refuse, of course!"

"Open that door! Do you hear me? You are mad!"

O'Hagan swung the monocle, and smiled upon the rapidly-breathing Haverley with undisguised contempt.

"Captain Haverley," he said, "Sir Roger Rundel is my friend; and whilst I live, any gay Lothario who seeks to gratify his vanity by compromising my friend's wife shall find at least one obstacle in his path. You will either hand me a written undertaking to secure a transfer to the 5th, vice Captain Macklin, invalided—leaving for Burma on the 19th—or remove that obstacle. You quit this room upon no other condition."

"Open the door!" roared Haverley, clenching his fists and grinding his teeth with animal fury. "Open the door! By God! I'll clap you in custody before another hour has passed!"

"If you decline," said O'Hagan, coldly, "I will ring for the door to be opened as you desire——"

Haverley drummed his right fist into the palm of his left hand and stamped upon the floor with his foot. He was literally gasping in his fury.

"—In order," resumed the chilly voice, "that my man may thrash you. I offer you, for the last time, the satisfaction of a gentleman——"

"Damn your impudent speeches! Open the door!"

Captain O'Hagan pressed the bell.

The door opened so suddenly and violently as to precipitate Haverley forward into the room. He recovered himself, turned, and sprang with a cry upon Donohue.

("Donohue," O'Hagan has informed me, "is not of course an adept of the *Higher* Arts of Jiu-Jitsu; but he has a pleasing proficiency in the more ordinary holds and falls.")

Donohue, then, met the attack in a novel way. He received Captain Haverley in a loving embrace. Then, like a teetotum, Haverley was spun right-about, and held, purple-faced, eyes starting hideously, with his arms locked behind him by the human manacle of Donohue's iron grip.

Donohue: "Yes, sir?"

"You have your instructions, Donohue," said O'Hagan—and passing the inarticulate Haverley, strode out of the room.

V.

REVELATIONS.

"THE worse a man's reputation," Bernard O'Hagan holds, "the more the women like him. In French comedy we find the jealous husband held up to ridicule—hence the superiority of the lover. Failing the sword, Ridicule, my boy, is the weapon to cut short the career of Gallantry."

Remembering this, let us accompany Captain O'Hagan to Lady Rundel's.

He was admitted. Following upon such an affair as that of the previous evening,

HE DEALS WITH DON JUAN

it is more than doubtful if another had enjoyed the privilege of admission. But Bernard O'Hagan is unused to refusals.

Lady Rundel received him with studied coldness. He bent low over her hand in his remote, courtly fashion.

"I have an explanation to offer of my conduct of last night," he explained blandly.

"I am curious to hear it!"

"That I do not doubt, Lady Rundel; for you must have perceived that I strongly disapproved of the man Haverley!"

She was caressing a miniature dog, but at that she glanced up, flushing.

"It is a pity," she began——

"It is!" agreed O'Hagan, toying with his monocle. "It is indeed a thousand pities, for you are such a charmingly pretty woman!"

"Captain O'Hagan! I fail to understand you!" But her eyes were less angry than her tones. "You presume too far, even for so old a friend, when you attempt to control my choice of acquaintances!"

"Dear Lady Rundel"—he bent forward and patted her hand soothingly—"it annoyed me so deeply (you know how acutely sensitive I am) to hear people laughing!"

"Laughing?"

Lady Rundel met his eyes interrogatively.

"I felt that the position was so very undignified. Sir Roger——"

"Captain O'Hagan—are you insinuating that people are laughing at my husband That——"

"At your husband! At Sir Roger!" O'Hagan stared amazedly through the pebble. "No one would dare to laugh at Sir Roger Rundel, believe me!"

A far-away look came into Lady Rundel's eyes at these words. O'Hagan was glad to see that look; glad for Sir Roger's sake. He knew, then, that his curious duty was almost accomplished—that Captain Haverley was merely a passing amusement.

Lady Rundel rose slowly from her chair. O'Hagan observed her slim figure with smiling, aesthetic appreciation. She walked across to a small table, glancing at some trifle

HE DEALS WITH DON JUAN 187

which it bore—and turned, leaning back upon the table-edge.

"What do you mean, then?" she asked. "At whom are they laughing?"

O'Hagan shrugged his shoulders with feigned embarrassment.

"A man who has been tarred and feathered," he began——

"Tarred and feathered!" Her eyes were opened widely. "Captain O'Hagan! Whatever do you mean?"

"——Casts ridicule upon any woman who consents to be seen in his company!"

"Captain O'Hagan, be so good as to explain yourself!"

O'Hagan raised his monocle.

"What! you did not know—about Haverley?"

"Frankly, I cannot believe it!" she cried, flushing deeply. "I am sure—I am almost certain—that Captain Haverley would not submit to such an indignity from *any* man!"

"It *is* an indignity, is it not?" he said, confidentially.

"Oh! I *cannot* believe it! And it is *known*?"

"That is the singular part of the thing! I have never been able to understand why Haverley did not remain abroad. It was my scamp, Donohue, who perpetrated the outrage!"

"Your *man*! Your man tarred and feathered Captain Haverley?"

"He did, the rogue! I would have discharged the fellow, but he is the only man in England who knows how to pack dress trousers in a suit-case!"

Lady Rundel was watching O'Hagan. When he really gets into his stride, my friend's mendacity is fascinating. He becomes supernormally fluent; his truthless discourse holds one enthralled.

"The car is ready," she said slowly. "I should like to hear this unsavoury story from the man Donohue himself!"

It was designed for a home thrust, but O'Hagan rose delightedly.

"Dear Lady Rundel," he said. "By all means You honour me."

VI.

DONOHUE AGAIN.

Some delay occurred at the door of O'Hagan's chambers.

"Donohue cannot have gone out," said he. "How careless of me to have forgotten my key!"

He rang impatiently. Once—twice—thrice. Then the door was opened some three inches and Donohue's face peered through the aperture.

"Excuse me, sir," said that treasure, ignoring O'Hagan's icy stare; "but would you, sir—I don't ask a favour often—would you come back in half an hour, sir?"

Captain O'Hagan thrust the door open, and swept Donohue against the wall.

"What do you mean?" he demanded fiercely. "Consider yourself discharged, Donohue! What . . ."

An uproarious banging and shouting drowned further speech. Lady Rundel clearly was afraid to enter. Donohue shrank away before the fierce glare which sought him through the pebble.

"*Donohue!*"—portentously.

"Sir!"

"What is that unseemly disturbance proceeding from the store-room?"

Donohue, with great hesitancy:

"I'm sorry, sir! You can discharge me if you like—excuse me, sir, you *have*! But he came here calling you such dirty names, sir, and—excuse me, m'lady—said things about her ladyship!——"

"Donohue!" interrupted O'Hagan, in a voice of freezing calm—"unlock the store-room door!"

"Sir——"

"Donohue! unlock the store-room door! Then pack your box."

Donohue, with a sort of badly veiled truculence—("I have always distrusted that man!" whispered Lady Rundel)—walked to and unlocked the door indicated.

Whereupon Lady Rundel uttered a stifled shriek.

For out into view leapt a nightmar

HE DEALS WITH DON JUAN

apparition—a man who had sky-blue hair and only half a moustache! Furthermore, that surviving half was grass-green!

"Come out, you piebald spalpeen!" cried Donohue, throwing restraint to the winds—"come out and show what I've done to you!"

Lady Rundel slowly raised her hands to her face.

"Heavens!" she said, in a smothered voice, "it is Bobby Haverley! Captain O'Hagan, your man must be given in char. . . ."

Her voice trailed off into a suppressed ripple.

"Lady Rundel!" shouted Haverley frantically—"This is a conspiracy! I have been lashed to a chair——"

But Lady Rundel already was half way down the stairs, and her laughter, no longer to be denied, came back in mocking answer. O'Hagan stood in the doorway, monocle raised. Haverley, by a tremendous effort, regained control of himself.

"Captain O'Hagan," he said, his voice

grating harshly, "you will be in jail to-morrow."

"Possibly," replied O'Hagan; "but let us survey the facts. If you care to give me the written undertaking to which I referred —merely a matter of form, *now*—you may enjoy the use of the hot and cold water in my bathroom. The dye will wash out. I will even lend you a razor. If you decline, you are at liberty to depart into Whitehall —as you are! Finally, Donohue has taken your photograph! You did so, Donohue?"

Donohue: "I did, sir."

"It will, of course, be reproduced in the press during the course of the case. The bathroom is on your immediate left."

Is it necessary to pursue this matter further? I think not. O'Hagan has not been prosecuted. He never will be, I fancy. Recently, he related to Lady Rundel the true facts of the affair; and I thought that she would have never ceased laughing.

Captain Bernard O'Hagan's policy is, Do it hard, and face the music. One sighs for a ministry of O'Hagans.

EXPLOIT THE SIXTH.

HE HONOURS THE GRAND DUKE.

EXPLOIT THE SIXTH.

HE HONOURS THE GRAND DUKE.

I.

WE MEET THE DUKE.

The character of my friend Bernard O'Hagan is a maze within a maze, a dædalian labyrinth, to the heart whereof I long since have despaired of penetrating. His sense of humour is acute, but peculiar. A man, he declares, who cannot laugh at Mark Twain is a man from whose soul the joy of life has departed. Yet his idea of bliss would seem to be existence in a Persian rose-garden with some few congenial spirits, and, for attendants, only Greek youths and maidens of flawless classic beauty.

Grotesque anomaly! For I defy any

philosopher to reconcile the ideals of Petronius Arbiter, Omar, and Samuel Clemens!

"Alas, O'Hagan," I say, "this world of ours is a grey place."

But he turns to me in surprise, monocle raised, and studies my face with a certain apprehension.

"How can you say so, Raymond? Have I not repeatedly demonstrated that Romance lurks in hiding amid the most prosaic surroundings? Adventure, my boy, is for the adventurous! It is only the blind who deny the existence of fauns. I will undertake to find you a nymph in any wood. Villains profound as the darkest dreams of Tolstoy regularly take tea in the drawing-rooms of Mayfair; heroes loftier than Charlemagne jostle one in the Strand!"

Potential Cleopatras and Trojan Helens, I take it, abound in London. Only lacking is that clash of Circumstance and the Man, which, in history, has cast up such wondrous beings.

As I glance at my picturesque friend,

head aloft, purple-lined cloak swung well back, and note the air of smiling defiance wherewith he faces the world, I perceive the *Man*, and with pleasurable anticipation await the Circumstance. I shall always remember one conversation of this kind, for the reason that it directly preceded our meeting with the Grand Duke.

We had just quitted the theatre. My proposal in reference to supper had discovered the interesting circumstance that our joint capital equalled three-and-nine.

"Had *you* come out without money," said O'Hagan, "I should not have been surprised. Had *I* come out without money I should not have been surprised. But for us both, on the same evening, to do so, reveals the finger of Fate."

O'Hagan, as he stood with one half of his face and figure lighted up by the glare of the theatre lamps, and the other blacked out in contrasting shadow, bore a resemblance rather more marked than usual to the Monarch of merry memory. Withal, he looked strikingly handsome. He is the only man of my acquaintance who can successfully wear a flowing, black dress tie.

Captain Bernard O'Hagan is a figure unforgettable.

"Well?" I said, impatiently watching the theatre-goers driving supperward. "Shall we have something at the club?"

"No, Raymond," replied my friend, reflectively. "That would be capitulating. Is it possible that two honourable gentlemen, chancing to be without half a sovereign or so, are forced to sup on credit? I recall an episode in the career of my ancestor, Patrick."

He is fond of recounting episodes in the career of this ancestor, Patrick—some time of the Musketeers of Louis XIII.—a gentleman who would seem to have been chiefly notable for suave ruffianism.

The nature of the episode I was not destined to learn, however, at the time; for as O'Hagan lighted a cigarette, a block in the traffic occurred at the corner of Wellington Street (do not misunderstand me to mean that the incidents were correlative); and a handsome limousine was held up immediately in front of us. The interior was brilliantly illuminated, and a gentleman who lounged upon the fawn-coloured cushions glanced curiously in our direction.

This gentleman, the sole occupant, was distinguished by fiery moustachios and a squarely trimmed beard. My association with what O'Hagan terms "the lower journalism" has familiarised me with the faces of notabilities.

"That is the Grand Duke John of Siresia," I volunteered, idly.

"So it is," said O'Hagan with lively interest. "So it is!"

And ere I could say another word he had stepped to the door of the car, opened it, and engaged the distinguished foreigner in conversation!

Whilst I knew O'Hagan's visiting-list to be extensive and peculiar, I hitherto had been unaware that he was acquainted with the Siresian autocrat. His action took me completely by surprise. Then, just as the policeman ahead released the pent-up traffic, my friend turned and beckoned to me.

Full of a great wonder, I joined him at the open door.

"Get in, Raymond!" he directed briefly, and thrust me, speechless with astonishment, into a seat opposite the great personage.

The chauffeur glanced back. The footman leapt down and came to the step. As in a dream, I heard rapid, guttural instructions. The footman saluted and leapt to his place. The car moved smoothly onward.

O'Hagan raised his monocle, gazing at the bearded nobleman; then waved it gracefully in my direction.

"You may not have met my friend, Mr. Lawrence Raymond," he said, with the lordly condescension which he, alone, knows how to assume. "Raymond—His Highness the Grand Duke John of Siresia!"

II.

WE IMPROVE THE ACQUAINTANCE.

O'Hagan's friendship is a passport from the commonplace to the amazing. In acknowledgment of this off-handed introduction I bowed, and was mute. The Grand Duke nodded. His eyes constantly sought my nonchalant friend.

"How fortunate," said the latter smoothly, "that the traffic chanced to be delayed."

Bewildered, utterly, I acquitted myself of an ambiguous nod.

"Where are they?" asked the Grand Duke suddenly. His delivery was thick, unmusical.

"If you will be good enough to glance rearward," replied O'Hagan, "you will perceive a car which is following closely!"

We were, at that moment, turning around by Trafalgar Square; so that this prediction impressed me as being a peculiarly safe one. The Grand Duke, however, peering through a little window at the back, turned again to O'Hagan with palpable uneasiness. His heavy, dull features marked him a man of bulldog tenacity and autocratic stupidity.

"A green car?" he inquired.

O'Hagan, twisting about one finger the black ribbon attached to his monocle, inclined his head gravely. The tone of the Grand Duke's query had been peremptory—that of one accustomed to command and to be slavishly obeyed. My friend's mode of reply—the graceful and dignified inclination of the head, the lowering of the eyelids—had subtly defined, and with exquisite artistry, his attitude toward the Grand Duke.

In that simple inclination he had conveyed: "Duke"—(it were impossible to imagine O'Hagan addressing any man breathing as "Your Highness")—"Duke, you are in the company of a gentleman at present amicably disposed toward you, but of a gentleman who would as promptly tweak your nose, should you forget what is due to him, as he would tweak any other."

It was a silent declaration of aristocracy, typically and peculiarly O'Haganish.

HE HONOURS THE GRAND DUKE 203

A faint shade of difference crept into the Grand Duke's voice. I doubt if the man has lived, since Napoleon Buonaparte, who, meeting Captain the Honble. Bernard O'Hagan, could have escaped enmeshment within his catholic patronage. O'Hagan would patronize the shade of Julius Cæsar.

"What," inquired the Grand Duke awkwardly, "do you propose?"

"First," said my friend, holding his monocle between second and third fingers, and waving it roofward, "extinguish these interior lights. It was most indiscreet to travel so publicly."

Association with Bernard O'Hagan renders one more or less accustomed to the *outre*. The amazing ceases to amaze, the appalling to appal; wonders lose their potency, and one's pulse remains normal amid singular adventures.

It afforded me small surprise to see my friend's injunction instantly obeyed. (It would afford me small surprise to see the Premier blacking O'Hagan's boots.)

"Next," continued the Captain, "direct your man to drive to your embassy."

The obedient Grand Duke bent forward and called gutturally into the tube.

("There is one thing," O'Hagan tells me, "which a nobleman of the Grand Duke's race can never appreciate—the doctrine of aristocratic equality. He must always dominate or be dominated. My ancestor, Patrick, had this from the lips of Cardinal Richelieu—a singularly shrewd observer, Raymond, and a gentleman.")

"I have no intention," resumed the Grand Duke, "of handing them over to the ambassador."

O'Hagan shrugged his shoulders impatiently, turning his eye-glass upon the speaker with the air of a wise man weary of folly.

"*Will* you allow me to advise?" he said, with a certain disdain. "Do *they* know that?"

"They cannot possibly," replied the other. "It is what they most fear—eh?"

"Very well, then," drawled O'Hagan, yawning discreetly under cover of a gloved

HE HONOURS THE GRAND DUKE

hand, "they will abandon the pursuit and no attempt will be made upon your private apartments."

"I do not fear their attempts!" growled the Grand Duke, with truculent contempt.

"My good Duke!" said O'Hagan languidly—"my dear Duke—do you wish every paper in Europe to discuss your affairs? Do you wish all the world to hear of an attempt to burgle your rooms?"

"What! do you think they would dare?"

Captain O'Hagan surveyed him, pebble uplifted, as one surveys a surpassing fool.

"Dare!" he said icily. "Dare! My good, dear Duke—where is your common sense?"

("That expression marked the psychological moment, Raymond," he later was good enough to inform me. "I was deliberately tightening the screw. If he submitted, I knew that the man was mine.")

The Grand Duke glared for a moment. Then:

"No; you are right!" he agreed, grudgingly.

Bernard O'Hagan would be a dazzling ornament to the diplomatic service. One can imagine his prevailing upon the united monarchies of Europe to present a fleet of dreadnoughts to Great Britain as a little token of esteem.

Is it necessary, by the way, that I mention here how all this extraordinary conversation was so much Sanscrit to me? I think not. I perceived no gleam of light through the darkness. I was a man in a tunnel leading he knows not whither, surrounded by he knows not what.

My bewildered surmisings had come to a hazy meridian, I think, when the car drew up before the embassadorial residence.

"If he is at home, what excuse shall I make for my call?" asked the Grand Duke.

"Any excuse!" said O'Hagan drily. "You may profess to have heard rumours that he is troubled with a return of his gout——"

"He has no gout!"

"His wife's gout, then! Anything—anything!"

Grunting uncouthly, the Grand Duke alighted and disappeared in the darkness. Coincident with the footman's reclosure of the door, burst forth my dammed up torrent of queries.

"*Ssh!*" O'Hagan raised his hand. "I will explain later, Raymond. Exhibit no surprise. Merely agree with me—tacitly agree!"

"But where did——"

"*Ssh!*"—impatiently. "These servants are spies!"

I felt curiously like a screw-stoppered bottle of some highly aerated mineral, which has been partially unscrewed. Questions literally *sizzled* from me. But I must perforce contain myself; and we were presently rejoined by the Grand Duke. He glanced up and down the street ere entering. Giving a brief order to the man:

"Where are they?" he growled, as he took his seat.

"They have left their car," replied my friend; "but two of them are in hiding near the corner."

"Do you know either of these?"

"*He* is one!" said O'Hagan impressively

"Whom?" snapped the Grand Duke.

Now, Captain O'Hagan is rarely at a loss for the right word at the right time. He holds it churlish to stammer and stutter, and wholly inconsistent with that grand manner of which, if I be not mistaken, he is the only surviving master. Yet, now, he seemed somewhat taken aback. Later, I understood why. But——

"Need you ask?" he returned, with very brief hesitancy.

"Not Leo?" the Grand Duke demanded, hoarsely.

O'Hagan smiled and inclined his head.

The Siresian nobleman struck his huge fist into the palm of his hand, furiously. He was a truly formidable man.

"Curse him ten thousand times!" he shouted, wildly. "How has *he* found out that I have them?"

"I fear you have been indiscreet, Duke," murmured O'Hagan.

"Indiscreet!" roared the Grand Duke.

"Not a living soul can have seen me meet Casimir! Ah, but——"

He broke off, evidently struck by a new idea.

"Was he followed?" he demanded.

"I fear so!" gravely answered my friend.

"They—have him?"—jerkily.

"I fear so!"

The Siresian swore, stormily.

"Ah, well," he concluded. "He was well paid for the risk—poor devil!"

And now we were in the heart of hotel-land. The car drew up before the dazzling portals of the New Louvre. The footman threw open the door and stood rigidly to attention. On the car-step the Grand Duke hesitated, turned, and was delivered of a new idea.

"Now that I have the letters and the photographs, what have I to fear?" he snapped, in an angry voice. "They cannot reach them here! And do they not think that I have delivered them to the embassy?"

O'Hagan placed a gloved finger to his lips, and directed a rapid glance through his monocle toward a hotel servant who stood immediately behind the footman.

"It is good of you to bring us along to supper, Duke!" he cried loudly and breezily. "Fancy running into you at the Folly of all places!"

The Grand Duke accepted the guidance of this accomplished diplomat. In single file we entered the hotel—the nobleman frowning thunderously at the liveried servant silently impeached of espionage by O'Hagan. To a suite of apartments furnished with opulent magnificence we made a stately progress. When, for a few moments, my surprising friend and I found ourselves alone, the mental volcano which raged within me burst into active eruption, casting forth questions in a burning torrent.

O'Hagan, hand raised: "My dear Raymond!"

I talked on, but diminuendo.

O'Hagan, raising monocle: "My dear fellow!"

The querulous torrent died away, *poco à poco*. Then:

HE HONOURS THE GRAND DUKE

"I had anticipated all your questions, my boy," said O'Hagan; "and I will deal with them in order. In the first place—No, I am *not* acquainted with the Grand Duke! I had never seen him in my life until you drew my attention to him outside the Folly! I have no idea what it is that he has secured, and which he evidently apprehends someone is likely to pursue him in order to recover!— letters and photographs, according to his own account. Do not glare in that way, Raymond; it makes you appear cross-eyed!"

To the door I looked hurriedly, and back to my nonchalant friend, who swung his monocle and eyed me with an amused smile. My tongue defied me.

"If you will glance over our conversation, in retrospect," he continued, "you will perceive that my contributions partook of the nature of leading questions disguised as items of information. In fact, I adopted the tactics of an examining magistrate!

"It all rests upon this, Raymond. At the moment when you said, 'That is the

Grand Duke John, you may recall that I was about to recount to you an exploit of my ancestor, Patrick? This exploit, Raymond, was performed before La Rochelle, and involved three of the enemy, a dozen bottles of wine, and a game pie! The Grand Duke is the enemy in this case, my boy. You must be aware that he is one of a group whose activities are inimical to our interests in the Baltic. I saw my way clearly. I stepped up and whispered to him, 'They are following you, Duke! We will slip into the car, unperceived amid the traffic, and explain more fully. There must be no delay here!'"

(I inhaled noisily.)

"This was a bow at venture, Raymond. The odds against my scoring were about ten thousand to one. But—as occurred to a certain Desmond O'Hagan on a somewhat similar occasion—I scored! Given such premises, who after that could err? Although I will confess that I overstepped the mark once; but, thanks to the darkness of the car, and the corresponding darkness

HE HONOURS THE GRAND DUKE 213

prevailing in the Grand Ducal mind, I recovered! I may add, Raymond, that our present position, though one of absorbing interest, is delicate to a degree!"

"O'Hagan!" I broke in hotly, "this is beyond belief! Had I known, had I dreamed, of the false position in which we were placed——"

I ceased. Language failed me again. Then:

"O'Hagan!" I cried, "what have you done it for?"

"Primarily," he answered, "for supper! After supper I shall offer the Grand Duke any satisfaction which he may desire. Secondarily, here *is* the Grand Duke!"

Even as he spoke my mind was busy; and, as I now perceived with consternation, O'Hagan had indeed been "pumping" the Grand Duke—"pumping" him with the cleverness of a very accomplished K.C. I was amazed; amazed that the Siresian should have fallen so easy a victim—that even Bernard O'Hagan should have had the stark effrontery to practise such a deception.

"If you will excuse me for a few moments more," said the Grand Duke, "I will rejoin you for supper."

With a cold bow, he left us again.

"O'Hagan!" I burst out——

O'Hagan coughed, and raised his monocle to his eye.

"—I will not, cannot stay!——"

O'Hagan coughed again, more urgently, and, across my left shoulder, seemed to focus something through the pebble.

"—The supper would choke me!"

O'Hagan coughed a third time, with bronchial violence, bowed low—as a Leicester before an Elizabeth—and surreptitiously kicked me shrewdly upon the shin.

I spun around sharply. I followed the direction of my friend's enraptured gaze. And my eyes rested upon one of the loveliest women I have ever seen!

III.

THE MAID AND THE RING.

I CALL her a woman, but she can have been no more than seventeen or eighteen, I think. She was one of those dark, supple Siresian girls who approach so infinitely nearer to one's ideal houri of the East than any really Oriental beauty ever can do. Her great black eyes wandered nervously from O'Hagan's face to mine.

"Tell me!" she cried, in pretty, broken English—"I saw you whispering together—tell me! You are from Leo?"

Nipping my arm, O'Hagan bowed again.

"I knew it!" cried the girl joyously. "Something told me!"

Good God! at her words, at sight of the mist of gladness, of gratitude, clouding her beautiful eyes, I could have kicked myself—I could have attacked O'Hagan nor counted the cost!

"He is so stupid—the Duke," she ran on, confidently: "so stupid! He leaves his coat in there"—she pointed to a distant door —" and these "—producing a bulky, sealed parcel—" in the pocket ! "

Then she laughed joyously. Her eyes, though, brimmed over with tears. Her credulity amazed me, of course; but not so greatly as one might suppose. There is something about O'Hagan that women trust implicitly; and it is something, I contend, which shall be written to his credit in the greater Doomsday Book—a real grandeur of soul which all his surprising superficialities cannot wholly mask.

Perceive me, then, at this juncture, a man rendered helpless by warring emotions, conflicting doubts, fears, and a supreme wonderment.

"Do you think you will be in time?" she pleaded, pressing the packet into his hands.

"I hope so, mademoiselle!" he replied.

His handsome face was stern. He had dropped his monocle, and, with it, I thought, somewhat of his flippancy.

"They may think he has turned traitor!"

she went on, rapidly : "*he*—who has given up everything to the Cause ! But they will be furious—they will not reason ! Even now, monsieur, they may be condemning him ! "

Her use of the word " monsieur " set me wondering. Her voice broke. Her brave eyes grew dim. And a lump rose in my throat. For I had perceived the reality of her trouble, and I think I had never felt a more despicable scoundrel. I thought that, as a man and a gentleman, I truly was not worth our united three-and-ninepence ! What should I do? How should I act ? Thus, miserably, I searched my inert intelligence ; then :

" Listen," began my friend, succinctly— " I cannot go among them, because I am not one of them ! Do not be afraid. I am a true friend to the Cause and to Leo. But how may I reach him ?—where do they meet to-night ? And are you certain that he will be there ? "

A shadow—a vague shadow—clouded the girl's face. Anxiously, intently, she watched O'Hagan ; and this he perceived.

" Mademoiselle," he said, with a frank

pride which is his peculiar birthright—" it is not possible that you can mistrust my word! Upon my honour, I will deliver this packet as you direct, and no man shall hinder me. But you must tell me where they meet, and how I may gain admittance."

A moment more she hesitated—searching his face with big, anxious eyes. Then dawned the light of a great resolution ; and I knew that she had determined to trust to her instincts.

"Here," she said, hastily pulling a ring from her finger. "Show this to the woman in the shop before the Café de l'Orient, Greek Street, and say 'Warsaw.' You will be admitted. Give the packet to Leo or to the President ; to no one else ! Quick ! go, I implore you ! "

O'Hagan took the ring, raised the girl's white fingers to his lips, and bowed over her hand as over the hand of a queen. It was the farewell of an old-time courtier and most perfect gentleman—completely untheatrical, exquisitely dignified. At such moments you perceive in my friend the ideal cavalier.

Her face flushed rosily—and paled to a greater pallor.

In the doorway O'Hagan turned again and bowed. Then, straight downstairs we hastened—he with the package in an inside pocket—and through to the street, unquestioned. A taxi-cab had just discharged a visitor at the door, and O'Hagan detained the man with a short, imperious gesture.

We leapt in.

"Café de l'Orient, Greek Street," said my friend. "Three-and-nine if you get there in five minutes!"

IV.

THE CONSPIRATORS.

THE cab having moved on,—

"I regret," began O'Hagan, "that we have missed our supper! But I have triumphantly proven my words anent the survival of Romance. You note into what a surprising adventure we have blundered merely by honouring a Grand Duke with our company! Here we have all the elements of a stirring romance indeed: the autocratic nobleman, the distressed lovers, the ring as a token! I am delighted, Raymond!"

"O'Hagan!" I interrupted sternly—"if *you* are delighted, I am appalled! Of the deception practised upon the Duke I will say nothing; but to have tricked a girl who confided——"

"Stop!" cried O'Hagan imperiously. "Stop there, Raymond! You!—my friend—and charge me with such a crime! Raymond!——"

"She thinks," I interrupted, excitedly——

"She thinks," my friend took me up, "that **we** are acquainted with her secrets, and trusts us accordingly. Good. Is her trust misplaced? Do we intend to betray her? No! ten thousand times no! It is perfectly evident that her lover—Christian name, Leo; surname, unknown; nationality, possibly Polish—is involved in some conspiracy directed against a government—probably that of Russia. Her father, or guardian, our mutual acquaintance the Duke, had obtained, through the treachery of one Casimir, proofs of Leo's complicity. These, we may assume, he intended to employ—(a) to frustrate Leo's designs in regard to the lady; (b) to bring about the arrest, or ruin, of the said Leo.

"Delightful, my boy! Wildly and picturesquely romantic! Enter Lawrence Raymond and Bernard O'Hagan—and what becomes of the ducal plan? It miserably crumbles to dust! Virtue and Love are triumphant, and we are the heroes of the hour!"

The cab stopped before a dingy little café. Our entire capital O'Hagan lavished upon the man, and we entered the café.

Its front portion proved to consist of a shop where coffee-pots and such utensils were sold, and behind the counter sat an adipose and unctuous lady of considerable maturity. O'Hagan's entrance brought her to her feet in quick alarm.

My friend held the ring before her eyes. She viewed it in palpable wonder, her slightly crooked gaze vacillating betwixt the face of my cavalierly friend and my own.

"*Warsaw!*" said O'Hagan, magnificently—and swept his arm toward a dirty glass-panelled door on our right.

"Oui, monsieur!" mumbled the old woman; and shuffled around the counter.

Without properly realising by what stages I had come there, I found myself standing before the closed door of an upper-floor room. O'Hagan knocked. A shouted conversation, rising, a harsh *duetto*, above an angry chorus, ceased abruptly.

O'Hagan threw wide the door and strode into the room.

This was small, smelling strongly of stale coffee and caporal cigarettes, and was illuminated by a gas burner low hung above a square table. About the table sat eight or ten foreigners—seemingly Russians or Poles—nearly all of whom leapt to their feet at our appearance. One, an old man with a venerable white beard, rose with greater dignity, fixing his brilliant eyes upon my friend.

O'Hagan rested one hand upon his hip, and with the other held the monocle an inch or so removed from his right eye. Amid a magnetic silence:

"Gentlemen," he said, with a sort of frigid courtesy—" and good people—you will favour me by resuming your seats!"

Of this gracious permission no one availed himself. An angry muttering arose, and—

"What is your business?" demanded the venerable chairman, in excellent English.

O'Hagan, through upraised glass, studied each face in turn and attentively. The muttering grew, and grew, and became a simian clamour. All eyes were turned to my nonchalant friend.

"My business, monsieur," he replied—speaking in French, probably with the idea that the rest of the company would be more likely to understand him—" is of the utmost gravity."

The uproar waxed louder. One swarthy, thickset fellow turned and took a step in

O'Hagan's direction. O'Hagan raised his glass again—and the fellow sat down.

"But," resumed my friend icily, "until a perfect silence is preserved I shall not disclose it" (louder uproar than ever); "I am not accustomed to interruption by the rabble."

Silence fell—save that it was a murderous silence. But:

"Your rebuke is just," said the aged spokesman, glaring fiercely around. "I will see to it that you are not interrupted. Your business, monsieur?"

"It is," replied O'Hagan, "to denounce a traitor!"

At that a perfect howl went up. Chairs crashed back upon the floor; and the discussion, which evidently had been interrupted by our entrance, was now resumed with renewed violence. All eyes turned upon a dark young man sitting on the right of the chairman. His handsome, aristocratic face was deathly pale, and his fine nostrils quivered with some emotion hardly repressed.

"Silence!" roared the chairman, in

clarion tones, and struck his fist upon the table with a resounding bang. "Silence! Are you mad, that you dispute with strangers present!" He glared about him ominously. "Again, monsieur"—to O'Hagan—"what is your business?"

O'Hagan paused awhile, staring down a man who continued to mutter rapidly to his right-hand neighbour. Then—

"The letters and photographs," began my friend, as one whose patience wearies——

But yet again he was interrupted, and now, by the dark young man; who leapt from his place, a hectic flush colouring his pale cheeks.

"You have them, monsieur?" he cried, holding his outstretched hands towards us. "God! you have them?"

O'Hagan:

"I have just recovered them from the apartments of the Grand Duke John!"

High heaven! Never can I forget the shriek of execration that greeted the name of the Grand Duke! We seemed, in a moment, to be surrounded by fiends of the uttermost darkness. They mowed and gibbered like animal things. Only the dark young fellow retained any self-control—sinking back upon his chair and biting his lip. But his eyes were glad; and by his eyes it was that I knew him for Leo.

"Silence!" came the mighty voice again. And the terrible old man glared about him, quelling his unruly compatriots like a pack of dogs. "Hand me those letters, monsieur."

O'Hagan, amid another throbbing stillness, produced the package.

"Am I addressing," he inquired, "the gentleman known as the President?"

"I am the President, monsieur," he was answered.

My friend passed the package to the old man. Rapidly, the latter broke the seals and examined the contents. Intense expectancy was written upon every face. It seemed that life or death hung upon the result of his examination. This, however was brief. Placing the bundle upon the table before him—

"Brothers," he said, with some emotion,

"a great danger is providentially averted. All are here!"

Something in his look suppressed the mighty shout almost ere it left the throats of the shouters.

"You said, monsieur," he continued, turning his eyes upon O'Hagan, "that you would denounce to us a traitor. I do not know who you are nor whence you come; but you have to-night done that which shows you a friend. You have saved the lives—and more than the lives—of some who never forget, and who will be grateful while they have hearts that beat. Your actions prove you: your words shall be respected. Name the traitor amongst us, monsieur."

The simple dignity of the old man's speech and manner impressed me immensely, but the eyes that glared from all around the table were not pleasant to see.

"For what I have done," said O'Hagan slowly, "I claim a reward: the immunity of the man I shall denounce!"

The necessity for the words was rendered evident by the negative yell which answered them; it was, however, immediately checked by the President.

"The reward you claim is a high one, monsieur," he said, "and wholly contrary to the rules of our Order! But the service you have rendered is beyond all human recompense. Therefore I grant your request."

Some few murmurs arose; but a glance from the fiery old eyes restored complete silence.

"The traitor," announced O'Hagan, "is called Casimir!"

"You lie!" screamed a man wearing a short, red beard, leaping madly to his feet. "Curse you! you lie!"

O'Hagan focussed him through the monocle.

"I was with the Grand Duke when you handed him the packet," he said, with a sort of suppressed ferocity—"you brick-dust baboon!"

"You were not!" shrieked the other. "The Grand Duke was alone——!"

He stopped. His florid face blanched to

a mottled white, and he dropped back, the picture of a rogue unmasked. Then:

"You see, monsieur," said O'Hagan to the President, "I have indicated your traitor and he has condemned himself; for the Grand Duke *was* alone!"

I expected a veritable pandemonium to burst upon us; but my expectation was not realised. The man seated beside Casimir turned, and with a cold smile, but blazing eyes, struck him deliberately across the face with his open hand. The outraged rascal bounded again to his feet; but a look around the silent company was enough. One quick glance he directed toward the old man, who stood with finger rigidly pointed to the door, and, head bent, he shuffled past us—and was gone.

Then, certainly, a scene of the wildest enthusiasm ensued. Everybody present seemed bent upon embracing Leo; but, escaping from his excited fellows, he came and took both O'Hagan's hands in his own, turning then to me, and shaking mine as warmly.

"Gentlemen," he said, in very fair English, "I will not attempt to thank you. I only thank God that there are such as you in the world!"

("Devilish embarrassing!" O'Hagan confessed to me, later, "considering the real objective of the expedition—*id est:* supper!"

"Here," said my friend, "is something to which you have a better claim than I." He handed Leo the ring. "To that brave lady you owe everything, sir; to us, nothing."

"She will always bless you," said the other, kissing the ring reverently—"as I bless her! I do not know your names, gentlemen—nor, in the circumstances, ask them. But if ever Fate should lead you to Poland, the home of Count Leo Riersiwicz is *your* home."

"Quite a charming little adventure," said O'Hagan, as we passed westward; "save that one cannot sympathise with any man who elects to associate with such a crew of undesirable pole-cats."

Two peers, a newspaper proprietor, and an actor-manager waited upon the kerb of Oxford

HE HONOURS THE GRAND DUKE

Circus, whilst 'bus drivers, draymen, vanmen on vans and other impossibles, drove by. O'Hagan's procedure on occasions of this kind is a joy unique and a memory ineffaceable.

Regardless of the direction, language, behaviour, or wishes of such persons, he proceeds across the road at the same dignified and even pace which he had observed upon the pavement. With dray horses standing on their hind-legs and waving their fore-legs over his picturesque head, with taxi-cabs menacing plate-glass windows, and motor 'busses hastily diverting their routes, he pauses to light an Egyptian cigarette.

Having returned his gold matchbox to his waistcoat pocket, unruffled he pursues his way, the only extant example of the *grand seigneur*.

The End

This edition is limited to 1,000 copies.

In Memoriam—Sax Rohmer
1883-1959